"I keep getting these subtle signals from you,"

Zach said, imprisoning her hand in his. "Maybe they're unconscious."

Darcy sat very still as his hand tightened around hers. The simple action felt so intimate, it took all her will to meet his gaze.

Was she sending out unintended signals? She couldn't deny that she felt drawn to him, that his closeness unsettled her and his touch made her panic and want to bolt before something disastrous happened.

"That's ridiculous," she said forcefully.

"Is it?" he said softly. "You keep fidgeting," he pointed out. "I've never seen you do that on television. You're as cool as a cucumber in front of the camera."

She felt anything but cool at the moment. She'd never felt this seductive, mesmerizing warmth that was stealing through her body.

Darcy sucked in a deep breath. "You're very good at seduction, Doctor."

Dear Reader:

No doubt you have already realized that there's a big—and exciting—change going on in Intimate Moments this month. We now have a new cover design, one that allows more room for art and has a truly contemporary look, making it more reflective of the line's personality.

And we could hardly have chosen a better month to introduce our new look. Jennifer Greene makes her second appearance in the line with *Devil's Night*, an exciting and suspenseful tale that still has plenty of room for romance. Old favorites are here, too. Barbara Faith's *Capricorn Moon* and Jeanne Stephens's *At Risk* show off these two authors at the top of their talent. Finally, we bring you a newcomer we expect to be around for a long time. Once you read Kaitlyn Gorton's *Cloud Castles*, you'll know why we feel so confident.

In coming months, look for favorites like Marilyn Pappano, Nora Roberts, Kathleen Korbel and Paula Detmer Riggs, as well as all the other authors who have made Silhouette Intimate Moments such an exciting—and romantic—line.

Leslie J. Wainger
Senior Editor

At Risk

JEANNE STEPHENS

Silhouette Intimate Moments

Published by Silhouette Books New York

America's Publisher of Contemporary Romance

SILHOUETTE BOOKS
300 East 42nd St., New York, N.Y. 10017

ISBN: 0-373-07308-9

First Silhouette Books printing October 1989

Printed in the U.S.A.

Books by Jeanne Stephens

JEANNE STEPHENS

loves to travel, but she's always glad to get home to Oklahoma. This incurable romantic and mother of three loves reading ("I'll read anything!" she says), needlework, photography, long walks—during which she works out her latest books—and, of course, her own romantic hero: her husband.

Chapter 1

Darcy Gilbert felt her mood shifting like the halos around the street lamps. Going from the television station to her regular Thursday-night destination was moving, literally and figuratively, from light to darkness. From heaven to hell in a few blocks.

A wet journey on this particular Thursday night. It was the third rain in five days, and since this was only the first week of October, there was speculation that they were in for an even wetter than usual season.

At eleven o'clock, traffic was light on Capehart Drive, a major artery through the city. Sounds were muted: an occasional hiss of tires on the wet street, a steady drumming of rain on car roofs. Headlights were reflected in shimmering circles on the dark, glistening pavement.

Darcy had the car heater running for the first time in months, and a faint smell of singed lint mingled

with the odor of wet leaves from the oaks and maples
lining the avenue.

Foleyville was usually hot and sticky in the summer, and in the winter the cold cut through clothing as
keenly as a newly honed blade. Like the entire Ozark
region, the city was best in the fall, when there was still
some summer mellowness in the air, and the sharp
winds had not yet started blowing down from the
mountains.

Already the leaves were turning, building to the
glorious display of colors that would culminate in late
October and bring the year's last crop of tourists to the
area. Just before Thanksgiving, Foleyville would settle down to being an ordinary middle-sized Arkansas
city, its craft shops closed until the spring craft fairs
brought the tourists back. In spite of the glut of tourists, Darcy loved Foleyville in October. She even liked
the gentle autumn rains.

She approached the lighted civic center square, and
her glance lingered on the graceful light-and-shadow
lines of the buildings, as if to store up a reserve of
beauty against the next few hours of ugliness and de-
spair.

On Thursday nights she worked a four-hour shift as
a volunteer on the Domestic Violence Hot Line.

She turned off Capehart Drive on Sixth and pulled
into the parking lot behind the old Victor Bank building. The bank had moved to the suburbs eight years
ago, and the building now provided office space for
several small, struggling businesses along with the DV
hot line.

A car pulled in next to Darcy's and Betina Meyer, also a volunteer, got out. Darcy joined her and they walked toward the building together, sharing Betina's umbrella.

"Saw both your newscasts this evening," Betina said. "You had the same news at six and ten." After three years as a weekend feature reporter, Darcy had, for the past year, been co-anchor of the evening news on a local TV station. It was the job she'd dreamed of ever since her freshman year in college. After twelve months, she knew the job wasn't perfect, but it was the nearest thing to it she'd found.

"We often do. Hadn't you noticed?"

Betina laughed her rough chain-smoker's laugh. "I sooi-ten-ly have," she said in an exaggerated Brooklyn accent. Originally from New York, Betina was one of the walking wounded, a survivor of a twenty-five-year abusive marriage that ended only when her husband died of colon cancer. Widowed, she had left her native environment with its bleak memories and moved to Arkansas, where she'd spent a couple of pleasant childhood vacations with her family.

"We just report the news. We don't manufacture it."

"Too bad."

"I must confess, on slow days like today, I'm tempted to do something drastic like read the headlines from supermarket tabloids. Ninety-year-old Woman Gives Birth to Quadruplets. She Didn't Even Know She Was Pregnant. Or, Woman's Head Transplanted to Man's Body. Patient Off the Critical List but Confused as Hell."

Betina cackled heartily. "I like it. I noticed a lulu yesterday. Man Raised with Chickens Grows Feathers."

Sobering, she added, "Too bad you can't report some of the true stories we hear on the hot line."

"We'd be accused of exaggeration and sensationalism."

Betina grunted in agreement. Most people didn't want to hear about domestic violence. They turned away from things that made them uncomfortable, taking refuge in the position that outsiders shouldn't interfere in "family squabbles." And when confronted with the alarmingly high domestic violence statistics, an amazing number of people simply refused to believe the numbers.

Darcy and Betina had discussed the widespread attitude often, from every angle. There was nothing left to say. Betina changed the subject. "That red blouse you had on tonight looked great on the screen."

"Vibrant colors always do," Darcy agreed.

They entered the building, which smelled of stale cigarette smoke and mildew, and climbed the stairs to the hot line's second-floor office. For privacy, there was no sign on the door. The square room was furnished with three long, metal tables. On each sat two phones, carrying four incoming lines. Only three of the phones were presently in use, and as Darcy and Betina entered, a young sociology student named Phil abandoned one and rose from his chair. The other volunteers, receivers pressed to their ears, waved silent greetings.

Phil grabbed a sweatshirt from the coatrack and pulled it over his head. "Boy, am I glad to see you guys." The words were muffled by the shirt. His head cleared the hole and he tugged the shirt down over his white T-shirt. "Higgins is sick so we're even more shorthanded that usual." In the background the phones rang repeatedly.

"Pretty hectic tonight, huh?" Betina queried, as she propped her umbrella against the wall.

Phil grimaced. "The natives are definitely restless. Must be a full moon behind the clouds."

"Nope," Betina said.

"Then it's the rain."

"Or the thinning of the ozone layer," Darcy commented. "Any excuse will do."

"I'd stay and help," Phil said, "but I've got a psych exam tomorrow and if I don't hit the books, I'm history in that class."

Betina pulled out a chair and reached for the nearest phone. "Go cram, Phil. Make your mother proud. We'll take it from here." She punched a lighted button and said, "Domestic Violence Hot Line. This is Mary." All the volunteers used pseudonyms on the hot line.

Darcy hung her jacket on the old-fashioned coatrack in the corner and took the nearest empty chair. She punched down a blinking button and reached for the receiver, but hesitated as she heard what Betina was saying.

"Take a deep breath, dear. There, that's better. Yes, Jo's here." She looked at Darcy and put her hand over the mouthpiece. "It's Claire Champlin. I can barely understand her, but she seems to want you."

Darcy had talked to Claire Champlin several times before. She nodded and punched down the appropriate button. "This is Jo, Claire. How are you tonight?" All she heard was muffled sobbing. "Are you at home, Claire?"

The woman finally gained enough control of herself to reply. "Yes."

"Are you in any immediate danger?" Volunteers were trained to determine, as quickly as possible, whether callers were in imminent need of protection. If so, and if an address could be obtained, the police would be called.

Claire choked back a sob. "No. He—Ralph just left for work. He was late."

Had to take time out to teach the little woman a lesson, Darcy thought bitterly. She remembered that Claire's husband was employed as a night watchman. "What happened? Can you talk about it?"

"He—he's been drinking all day—he—" She broke into hopeless sobbing.

"Claire, listen to me," Darcy said gently. "You don't have to talk about it now, if it's too difficult for you. You can call me back later, when you're calmer."

"No—no!" She sounded panicked, as though Darcy's voice represented her single, fragile hold on sanity. "I have to talk to somebody now. Don't hang up! Give me a minute, please."

"Take your time. I'll wait." Darcy ran long fingers through her damp hair and closed her eyes in an effort to shut out the drone of conversation going on around her. So many people living with violence, she reflected, feeling they had nowhere to turn except an anonymous voice on the other end of a telephone line.

Claire made a gulping sound. After a few moments, she said, "I shouldn't have said anything about his drinking, I guess."

"Shouldn't you say whatever's on your mind?"

"I don't know . . . I worry that he'll get fired, going to work like that—but, no, I shouldn't have said anything. It always makes him mad when I say he drinks too much."

Translation: It's all my fault. Typical reaction of many battered women. Darcy stifled her frustration. "He wasn't mad before that?"

"Well, yes. He was mad because the meat loaf was burned."

"So, you first noticed he was angry at dinner, when he saw the meat loaf was burned?"

Claire blew her nose. "Not really. He got up in a bad mood. I guess he'd have been mad no matter what I did."

Good, Darcy thought. A journey of a thousand miles begins with a single step. "I've gotten up on the wrong side of the bed myself a few times, haven't you?"

"Sure, I guess so."

"When that happens, what do you do?"

"I go out and work in the yard."

"You don't punch one of your children? Or a neighbor?"

"Of course not! It's not their fault I'm in a foul mood."

"Exactly."

There was a brief silence. "I know what you're saying. I—oh, God, that hurts—" She made a whimpering sound. "I'm sorry. I moved my arm. I think he broke it."

Darcy sat forward in her chair. "Claire, you need to see a doctor."

"No." She gasped. "I can't leave the house. Ralph always calls me two or three times to make sure I'm here."

"If your arm is broken, it has to be set."

"There's no one to stay with the kids," Claire said, her voice dull with impotency.

"Isn't there anyone you can call?"

"Well, there's my next-door neighbor, but what would I tell her?"

"Don't tell her anything." Darcy doubted the neighbor needed to be told. She probably knew what was going on next door and had chosen not to get involved. "Just say you have to go out for a while."

"I don't have a car."

"Call a cab."

"I don't have any money."

Claire had sucked her into the yes-but game, Darcy realized. No matter what suggestion she made, Claire would counter with a "yes, but" to explain why it wouldn't work. So she had to end the game now.

"Let me see if I have this straight. You're going to sit in your house and endure excruciating pain and let your arm grow permanently crooked or get gangrene or God knows what because there's absolutely nothing else you can do?"

Claire was silent so long Darcy began to think they'd been disconnected. Finally Claire quavered, "If you'll come and get me, I'll go to the hospital."

Volunteers were warned not to become personally involved with callers. Remaining emotionally detached was considered so important that they hid behind false names. That wasn't the only reason for pseudonyms, of course. They also provided protection against the occasional irate or psychotic caller who might decide he had a score to settle with a volunteer.

Darcy understood the valid reasons for the no-personal-involvement rule, but every rule had its exceptions, and she decided this was one of them. "Give me your address," she said and wrote it down as Claire dictated. "I'll be there in twenty minutes."

As Darcy hung up, Betina, who was lighting a cigarette between calls, gazed at her with narrowed eyes. She took a deep drag on the cigarette and blew smoke out of her nose. "Tell me I didn't hear what I think I heard."

Darcy stood and grabbed her jacket from the coatrack. "Her husband, Ralph, broke her arm."

"Good old Ralph," Betina muttered.

"It's the third time. She won't go to the emergency room unless I take her."

"What happened to rule number one?" Betina asked. "Never, repeat never, become personally involved with a caller."

"There are few nevers in life," Darcy said, retrieving her purse from the floor beside her chair. "Sorry to leave you shorthanded."

Betina blew smoke slowly toward the ceiling. "We're used to it."

"I'll come back if there's time after I take care of Claire." The other two volunteers were watching her now. Darcy's brown-eyed gaze swept the three of them. "Look, guys, you don't have to mention this to the director. Okay?"

"Be careful," Betina called as Darcy reached the door.

"Not to worry," Darcy told her. "Good old Ralph works nights."

Claire Champlin lived in a block of modest frame houses not far from County General Hospital. The porch light was on. The rain had thinned to a fine mist, and the pungent smell of damp earth was strong. Darcy picked her way across the soggy yard and knocked on the door. After several moments, the door eased open a crack and a thin, pale woman peered out. "Jo?"

"Yes. Are you ready to go?"

She opened the door wider. Her left arm was held at an awkward angle. "I sent the kids next door, and I just talked to Ralph, so maybe he won't call again until I get back. I have to get my purse."

She came back shortly and stepped out on the porch, leaving the porch light on. She looked intently at Darcy. "I've seen you somewhere. Have we met before?"

Now that Darcy had a better look at her, she saw a tall woman, so thin that her neck appeared too fragile to support her head. Her light blond hair was pulled back with barrettes on either side. There were lines around her eyes and mouth, not deep, but enough to show she was in her late thirties, maybe early forties. A streak of dark, coagulated blood sealed the slit in her bottom lip, and her left eye was swollen and discolored. Her expression was one of stoic acceptance, an expression Darcy had seen on other battered women. Claire wore a plain cotton dress with a light-colored windbreaker thrown over her shoulders.

"No, we haven't met. I'm Darcy Gilbert, Claire. I use the name Jo on the hot line in order to remain anonymous."

Claire took a quick, startled breath. "Oh, now I know where I've seen you. On TV. You're—" Suddenly Claire went white. Gasping, she sagged against the porch railing. A sheen of sweat glistened on her forehead. "My arm—the tiniest movement hurts so bad...it's the worst yet, I can tell...I took four aspirin tablets, but they didn't ease the pain."

"Can you make it to the car? I'll help you. I'll hold on to your other arm."

Claire nodded. She gathered her strength and moved gingerly to the porch steps. Once they were in the car, Darcy eased away from the curb. "I'll drive slowly and try to avoid jarring you."

"Thank you," Claire murmured. She let her head fall back against the seat.

"You all right?"

Claire nodded, but her expression seemed to say it didn't matter one way or the other. "It's nice of you to do this." She turned her head to peer at Darcy.

"What's somebody like you doing on a domestic violence hot line?"

Darcy kept her eyes on the road. "We have volunteers from all walks of life."

"But isn't it terribly depressing? Why do you do it?"

"I guess I feel I've been lucky. I have a job I love, a good life. It's my way of giving back something, helping other people in some small way." Darcy felt Claire studying her and kept her gaze averted. "Here's the turnoff for the hospital. There's a traffic bump. I'll take it slow and easy."

The car crept across the bump. Claire shut her eyes and groaned.

"Sorry." Darcy pulled up near the trauma-center entrance. "They'll give you something for the pain. You'll feel better very soon."

Darcy went around and opened Claire's door. Claire turned sideways on the seat and got carefully to her feet. "Maybe," she said in a defeated monotone, "they'll make a mistake and give me so much dope I'll go to sleep and never wake up."

"Self-pity is a waste of energy that could be better used to improve your situation."

"Oh, yeah?" Claire snorted. "How would you know?"

Darcy ignored the sarcasm and went ahead of Claire to open the door. There were several people in the large waiting room; most of them wore the strained, expectant look compounded half of hope and half of dread that can be seen in hospital waiting rooms anywhere. They all glanced up sharply as Darcy and

Claire entered, then looked away again when they saw the two women weren't hospital personnel.

A receptionist in a white pants suit came out from behind a glass-enclosed cubicle. "May I help you?"

"My friend is injured," Darcy said. "We think her arm's broken."

The receptionist led Claire to one of the curtained areas lining both sides of a long hall off the waiting area. Choosing a chair away from the other occupants of the room, Darcy shrugged off her jacket. She took out a compact and pulled a comb through her shoulder-length brown hair, then made a couple of passes at her mouth with lip gloss.

Two women across the room looked at her curiously and exchanged whispered comments. Evidently they recognized her. Darcy hoped they didn't try to strike up a conversation. She was too tired to chat with strangers. She turned away.

The clock on the wall said twelve thirty-three. She slid down in the chair, rested her head on the padded back and let her eyes drift closed. Within moments, she had fallen into a light doze.

She was in a dark room with a single window through which pallid moonlight pooled on a bare wood floor. She was intensely alert, attuned to the slightest sound. She moved to the window and opened it, intending to climb out. But there were bars, too close together to squeeze through. She backed away, feeling a flutter of alarm.

Running her hand along the wall, she searched for a door and, as seconds passed and the door eluded her, her anxiety grew. Was there such a thing as a room

without a door? She moved faster, sweeping her hand
in huge circles over the wall.

She was going to scream. She could feel the sound
gathering in her chest, pressing upward into her
throat. At the last moment before the scream broke
from her mouth, her hand touched wood—a door. She
found the knob and wrenched it right, then left. The
door was locked.

She whimpered and sagged against the door in de-
feat. Then she heard footsteps on the other side of the
door, coming closer, closer... Fear made her heart
race.

She knew who was coming. She crept away from the
door, hugged the wall, tried to shrink, disappear. The
footsteps stopped and the doorknob rattled. The
sound of a key being fitted into the lock was loud in
the silence.

Something terrible was going to happen...

She had to get out of there before the door
opened...

She had to...

Zach strode across the waiting room, bone-weary
from a ten-hour shift of patching up patients until the
family doctor or the appropriate specialist could take
over. Three car-wreck victims, a gut-shot teenage boy
who'd been showing off with his father's "un-
loaded" revolver and now clung to life by a thread,
two coronaries and a perforated ulcer. For the last
hour or so he'd been on automatic pilot, fueled by
habit and black coffee.

The receptionist had informed him that the TV anchorwoman Darcy Gilbert had brought in the Champlin woman. Zach scanned the room twice before he saw the top of a dark head above the back of a chair.

She was asleep, her legs drawn up beneath a full, navy skirt. Her cheek rested against the chair. Her dark hair, rumpled and falling over her forehead, gave her a look of childish innocence, of defenselessness. Black eyebrows arched delicately above dark lashes that cast shadows on high cheekbones. Her nose was straight and elegant, her mouth full and softly curved in sleep.

He had seen her many times on the television screen, but she was even more arresting in the flesh. She was a beauty, by any standard, and he was sure she couldn't walk down a street unnoticed, especially not if there were any men around.

Her body was slender and graceful. Her red silk blouse was molded to the curve of high breasts. A hand attached to an incredibly fragile-looking wrist lay, palm up, in her lap. The long, elegant fingers were faintly curled, the nails the same crimson color as her blouse. It was her left hand and ringless, he noted.

She must be very tired to have fallen asleep in that hard, vinyl chair; hospital waiting-room chairs were notoriously uncomfortable. It seemed a shame to wake her, and for a moment longer Zach made no move to do so. He found that he enjoyed watching her sleep and he felt an intense curiosity about this woman he'd seen so many times before but who'd never seemed real until now.

Her eyelids fluttered without opening, and she stirred and made a soft, murmuring sound. She must be dreaming. "Miss Gilbert?" he said quietly, but she slept on. He hesitated, then stretched out his hand to touch her shoulder lightly. "Miss Gilbert."

Her hand jerked up as if to ward off danger. "No!" Her eyes flew open, large, dark-chocolate eyes that remained dazed for an instant. Then she sat up, abruptly and fully awake. For another instant, there remained in her eyes a fear that went with the no she'd uttered as she'd passed the border between sleeping and waking. But the fear faded so quickly he wondered if he'd imagined it. She was looking up at him expectantly.

"I'm sorry if I startled you, Miss Gilbert." He offered his hand. "I'm Dr. Shaffer—Zach Shaffer."

She stood. Her hand was cool and dry, her grip firm, but he was surprised by how fragile the long, manicured fingers felt in his. In fact, she was smaller in general than he'd expected from seeing her on television, not more than four or five inches over five feet, and she couldn't weigh much more than a hundred pounds, a hundred and ten at most.

In spite of her delicate build, as she withdrew her hand from his, she no longer seemed defenseless. Instead, she appeared alert, composed, guarded. As a local celebrity, beautiful enough to have been successful in film acting, she probably had men falling over each other to get to her, he thought. Could any woman with all that going for her escape some measure of aloofness, even conceit?

Darcy regained her composure quickly. He had frightened her, leaning over her to rouse her from a disturbingly menacing dream. She'd come awake to find herself staring into a pair of penetrating blue eyes that seemed to fill her field of vision. She'd thought him a giant. She'd come to her feet, thinking that, standing, she wouldn't feel so small. But he was still huge, at least six three, broad-chested and long-armed. The sleeves of his white coat were too short, exposing thick wrists with a light dusting of auburn hair.

His chestnut hair was cut short, a lock falling over his broad forehead. There were weary lines around his eyes. He was, she judged, in his mid-thirties. His thick eyebrows were the same reddish-brown color as his hair and lashes, though the lashes faded to gold at the ends. He had an angular face, distinct cheekbones and faintly hollow cheeks, a long, straight nose. His mouth was wide and set firmly, his jaw square, his chin cleft. He wasn't handsome in the classical sense, but nonetheless striking.

Folding her arms across her breasts in an unconscious gesture of self-protection, Darcy asked, "How is Claire Champlin?"

"Resting comfortably. I decided to let her sleep while I spoke to you. The ulna is broken. We set and cast the arm, and I took a couple of stitches in her lip."

"Will you be keeping her overnight?"

"It isn't necessary, and I don't think she'd stay in any case. Before she fell asleep she seemed extremely anxious to get home."

"I know." She thrust her hands into the deep pockets of her skirt.

"Are you related to Mrs. Champlin?"

"No, just a—friend."

He watched her carefully, wondering if she was as tense as she appeared. Some people found hospitals threatening. But maybe she was just worried about her friend. "Look, would you like a cup of coffee? I could use one, and I'd prefer to talk privately."

He saw the hesitation before she said, "Yes, all right."

He touched her arm lightly to guide her toward a small staff room. She tensed instinctively, then relaxed with an effort. She still found his sheer physical size and strength daunting, and she'd been completely unprepared for his touch. Somehow the light physical contact of his hand at her elbow emphasized his maleness even more. Carefully she withdrew her arm and moved ahead of him as they entered the staff room.

The room contained three square tables, a small refrigerator, a microwave oven, a soft drink machine and a coffee maker. He filled two Styrofoam cups and carried them to the table where she sat. They were alone in the room.

Zach heaved a tired sigh and sprawled in his chair. Raising his cup in his big hand, he tasted the hot coffee. He studied her. "How long have you known Mrs. Champlin?"

"Not long."

He lowered his cup and regarded her for a moment, as though he were weighing his next words. "Tell me what happened tonight."

"Didn't Claire tell you?"

"She said she fell off the porch."

Darcy's brows rose. "Oh."

His blue eyes seemed to slice right through her. "We both know that's not what happened."

There was something accusatory in his tone, and Darcy shifted uncomfortably as she tried to decide how much she could reveal. The last thing she wanted to do was cover up for Ralph Champlin, but there was the problem of confidentiality between hot line volunteers and their callers.

"I've seen her before," he said, "about six months ago. It was her right arm that was broken then, and she said she fell out of an apple tree. Very accident-prone lady, Mrs. Champlin."

Darcy looked into her cup as she lifted it to her mouth. "I see."

He sat forward so suddenly that she instinctively drew back. This seemed to irritate him. "What do you *see*? Look here, Miss Gilbert, I strongly suspect this woman is being battered. By her husband, I presume. Why are you protecting him?"

"I'm not, but—"

He cut her off. "I'm going to have to report it this time."

Darcy's eyes widened in surprise. "You mean no report has been filed before this?" There seemed little point in trying to maintain confidentiality when he obviously already knew the score. "Are you aware that this is the third time her arm's been broken?"

"I wasn't until I looked back through her chart tonight. I wasn't on duty the first time she came in." He was puzzled by her indignant tone. "You're her friend, Miss Gilbert. If you've known all along what's going on, why haven't *you* reported it?"

Darcy bristled. He'd taken offense at her implied criticism. He could dish it out but he couldn't take it. "I only met Claire tonight. Before that, I talked to her on the telephone a few times. When she called tonight, I made sure she was in no immediate danger of further battering. Beyond that, I'm supposed to help Claire take charge of her own life while avoiding any personal involvement."

"That sounds like double-talk," he said, obviously impatient with her explanation.

"I'm a volunteer on the Domestic Violence Hot Line, every Thursday night from eleven to three," Darcy added. "I'm breaking a rule, being here."

Zach raised an eyebrow. There was more to her than a pretty face. He might have imagined her doing something highly visible, like pushing a cheer cart around the maternity ward of the hospital once a month. Never would he have suspected she'd volunteer for something so emotionally draining. She'd even driven to Claire Champlin's house after midnight and delivered her to the hospital. She could have dumped the woman and gone home to bed, but she had waited, obviously concerned. "Then why are you here?"

She shrugged. "She wouldn't agree to come to the hospital unless I brought her. So I decided to make an exception to the rule against personal involvement."

"She seems to trust you. Can you get her to tell the truth?"

"I doubt it. Please don't tell her we've talked about this, or she may never confide in me again."

"Was her husband at home when you picked her up?"

Darcy shook her head. "He works nights. She had to wait until he left before she could call me. She's terrified he'll call while she's away and be angry again. That's why she's so anxious to get home."

He looked at her in bewilderment. "When he sees the cast, won't it be fairly obvious where she's been?"

"Of course, but if he calls and she doesn't answer, he might assume she's out with another man. He'll have hours to work himself into a rage before he finds out where she really went."

"And she covers up for him!" He dragged a hand through his thick hair in a gesture of total frustration. Then he slammed his big hand down on the table hard. "I don't get it."

"Well, I doubt that I could explain it to you. Not in a few minutes' time." She pushed back her chair and rose abruptly, "Can Claire leave now?"

"Anytime."

"I'll try to get her to go to a shelter. Thank you for the coffee, Dr. Shaffer." She gave him a terse nod before she left.

With hooded eyes, he watched her walk briskly down the hall away from him. Her navy skirt whirled around long, shapely legs. Now, what had he said to make her cut him short and decide to leave so suddenly?

She seemed to feel he'd been negligent, not reporting Claire Champlin as a suspected battered woman the first time he saw her. At the time, it had seemed a simple broken arm. There were no other visible marks on her, as there had been tonight, so he'd accepted her story about falling out of a tree. He'd heard far more bizarre stories than that from accident victims. But Darcy Gilbert evidently thought his acceptance in the Champlin woman's case made him naive or uncaring.

Not an auspicious introduction to a woman he'd like to know better. It had been a long time since he'd met someone who made such a strong impression on him, and it wasn't merely her obvious physical assets. She was deeply compassionate, for one thing. Her choice of volunteer work and her attitude toward the Champlin woman made that clear. He was curious about other aspects of her personality that had remained hidden during their brief encounter. Darcy Gilbert had an aura of mystery about her. She intrigued him.

On the other hand, maybe he was just overly sensitive tonight. Certainly he was exhausted.

Sighing, he rubbed his hands over his face, feeling the rough stubble on his jaw. He needed a shave, shower and about ten hours of sleep. But he'd agreed to take an extra half shift and would be on duty for another two hours. He'd better keep moving.

He smothered a deep yawn and left the staff room.

Chapter 2

Claire was waking up when Darcy entered the examining room. She struggled awkwardly to sit up. Darcy lowered the bed's safety rail and helped her.

"What time is it?"

"One-thirty," Darcy replied.

Claire ran her tongue over her lips. "I feel dead-headed, like I'd been asleep for hours."

"That's the medication they gave you."

"Whatever it was, it stopped the pain."

"Good. Do you feel like getting on your feet?"

"Yeah." She slid off the bed and looked around dazedly. "Where's my jacket?"

"Here." Darcy plucked the windbreaker from a chair and draped it over Claire's shoulders. "Do you have to fill out any forms?"

"No, I gave them our health insurance information. They said that's all they needed."

Darcy waited until they were in the car to broach the subject of the shelter. "What would you think about not going back home for a few days? I can take you to a woman's shelter. It's called Hope House. You can remain there incognito for as long as you want to stay."

Claire was a bit slow to react, which Darcy put down to the painkiller she'd been given. Finally she reverted to form and began to throw obstacles in the path of Darcy's suggestion. "I have to pick up the kids."

"Surely there's someone you could call who'd pick them up and keep them a few days."

"Well, my mother lives here, but I hate to impose on her."

"I'll bet she'd be glad to help. You could call her from the shelter. In a day or two, if you decide to stay, you can have the children with you."

Claire uttered a heavy sigh. "Ralph would pitch a fit if he came home and I wasn't there. And I have to face him sooner or later, don't I?"

"How will he feel about your going to the hospital?"

"He'll be mad about that, too. But I think it'll be okay when he finds out I didn't tell the doctor how my arm got broken."

"As long as he's going to be angry, anyway..." Darcy let her voice trail off, knowing that she was verging on coaxing Claire to do something she might not be ready for. It had to be Claire's decision to take refuge at the shelter or she wouldn't stay.

Darcy started the engine and backed out of the parking space. "I know it's none of my business. I just want you to know you have options."

After a moment, Claire said hesitantly, "It'd be nice to be by myself for a while, so I could think."

"Yes," Darcy observed noncommitally.

They traveled a block in silence before Claire said, "Like you said, Ralph's going to be mad, anyway."

"Mmm."

"My mother's always after me to leave Ralph. Under the circumstances, I don't think she'd mind keeping the kids."

"You're lucky she lives in Foleyville."

A block later, Claire made up her mind. "I think I will go to that shelter, just for tonight—if it's not too much trouble."

"No trouble at all." At the next corner, Darcy altered her route, heading across town to Hope House, an ordinary six-bedroom brick residence that, on the outside, resembled the other large family homes in the area.

The housemother was used to being awakened in the middle of the night to take in the refugees of domestic wars. Darcy hoped that by morning, Claire would have decided to stay longer than one night and become involved in the house's group counseling sessions. But, again, it had to be Claire's decision.

It was after two by the time Darcy left Hope House. She stayed long enough for Claire to phone her mother, who agreed to pick up the children at the neighbor's house immediately, and to see Claire settled in her room.

Not unexpectedly, Claire had begun to doubt her decision. Darcy made haste to leave before the woman could talk herself into going right back home. Darcy promised to look in on her the next day. Hoping it would make Claire feel a little more secure, Darcy wrote her unlisted phone number on a scrap of paper and gave it to her.

Since her hot-line shift ended at three, anyway, she decided to go straight home. She'd been privy to enough pain and suffering for one night.

The rain had stopped. Driving through near-deserted city streets, Darcy tried to deal with her feelings about Claire's situation. It mattered a great deal to her that Claire find the strength to make positive changes in her life. It seemed she was getting too deeply involved in Claire's problems, after all. Perhaps some degree of emotional involvement was inevitable. She saw too much of herself in Claire.

She'd been the only child of older parents who had, years before Darcy's birth, adjusted to the idea of remaining childless. The two of them had built a satisfying life together, and by the time Darcy came on the scene, she was a disruption, an intrusion. They hadn't known quite what to do with her.

Her parents had done their best, but Darcy's memories were of feeling an outsider in a silent house. At night, after she'd been sent to bed, she'd heard her parents' murmured conversation until she fell asleep, conversation that for some reason they saved until they were alone. She didn't doubt that they cared for her, in their undemonstrative way, but she had not felt loved.

Lonely and insecure, she'd been poised to fall headlong in love with the first man who paid her the slightest attention. That man turned out to be Bill Bainbridge, whom she met the summer after her graduation from high school. He was handsome and charming, and to a shy, unhappy eighteen-year-old he seemed devastatingly worldly and exciting. They were married in September; Darcy was still three months shy of her nineteenth birthday.

She had seen evidence of Bill's quick temper almost from the first, but to a girl who'd been raised in an atmosphere where emotions were suppressed, she'd been drawn to Bill's volatility. His fiery temper and excessive jealousy on the one hand and his extravagant declarations of love on the other had made him seem so real, so *alive*.

She was later to realize that verbal abuse started soon after the wedding. They'd been married a year before the abuse accelerated to the point where he struck her. Her face had carried the marks of that first beating for days. Afterward, he was desperately contrite. He had apologized over and over with tearful pleas for forgiveness.

In her ignorance and need to believe him, she'd accepted his apology and tried to put the incident behind her. After all, he did love her. Didn't his tears prove it? It was as he'd said, she told herself: in his rage, he hadn't known what he was doing.

Still, it troubled her that she couldn't pinpoint the cause of such violent anger. He'd snapped at her over something trivial, and she'd snapped back. On the surface, that seemed to have triggered the attack. But the reaction was so out of proportion to the cause that she convinced herself the problem was his job. He was under too much stress at work; it was little wonder his control had snapped. The explanation for the attack thus settled in her own mind, she decided never to think about it again.

Bill hit her again six months after the first attack, and again the incident was followed by a surfeit of tears and apologies. The third time came just three weeks later.

Looking back on it now, Darcy realized it was a small miracle that she'd been able, at that point, to face the facts: the battering wasn't going to stop, no matter how many times he promised it would.

Since then, she'd listened to dozens of battered women, in counseling groups and on the hot line, and almost to a woman they lived lives of self-deceit, convinced there was something they could do to end the abuse. If only they were better cooks or housekeepers. If only they could lose weight. If only they didn't nag so much. If only they could somehow convey to the men in their lives how much they cared.

If they stayed in a violent relationship long enough, they eventually became helpless victims. Like Darcy in her dream tonight, they were confined in rooms without doors. Most of them needed a great deal of support to break out. If Darcy had stayed with Bill, she knew she'd have ended up as impotent and terrified as Claire Champlin.

Yet from somewhere, at twenty and with no knowledge of the dynamics of battering relationships, Darcy had found the courage to look at her marriage objectively, and she had left Bill.

If she hadn't immediately sought counseling, she'd probably have given in to Bill's fevered pleas and gone back to him. Claire was going to need counseling, too, and she wouldn't get it unless she stayed at the shelter.

Ralph Champlin would turn the city upside down looking for his wife. If he succeeded in finding her, he'd convince her things were different this time—he couldn't live without her, he'd learned his lesson, he'd never lay a hand on her again. Men like Ralph and Bill could be so sweet and eager to please, they could charm the birds out of the trees. Outsiders who saw only this side of them were convinced they were as near to ideal husbands as mere men could ever be.

Reflecting upon how easy it was to be misled by the front people show to the world, Darcy drove into her covered parking spot in the lot next to her apartment building. First impressions, she mused as she got out of her car and walked through the brisk autumn chill toward the building's lighted foyer. Although the rain had stopped, the night air remained pregnant with its smell.

First impressions should always be questioned, she thought as she stepped into the foyer. She called hello to the security guard behind the desk and passed into a long hall. Her apartment was on the east side, at the back of the building.

She unlocked the door and entered. She'd left a lamp on in the living room. The soft light was warm and welcoming. Too tired to do anything but hang up her clothes and remove her makeup, she slid between clean sheets with a sigh of gratitude.

If first impressions should always be questioned, she reflected as her eyes drifted closed, then maybe she'd been too quick to judge Dr. Zach Shaffer. She'd thought him a bit too sure of himself, a touch arrogant, not unheard of among the doctors she'd had dealings with. He seemed so confident, yet it evidently hadn't occurred to him until tonight to file a report with the police on Claire as a suspected victim of battering. It had taken three broken arms... Well, to be fair, he hadn't known about the first one before tonight.

Still, medical personnel should be more sensitive to possible domestic violence cases. Too many of them lacked not only knowledge, but also sympathy for battered women. She'd automatically put Zach Shaffer in that category, and maybe she'd judged too harshly. But, darn it, he'd cinched it when he'd said, "I don't get it," in total bewilderment. She'd known exactly what he meant—he couldn't comprehend why Claire stayed with a husband who beat her.

It seemed to be most people's automatic reaction. "Why doesn't she just leave?" they asked blithely, as if the solution were so simple.

Flopping over on her side, Darcy tried to make her mind a blank. She would never get to sleep if she didn't stop stewing about people who offered simple solutions to complex problems or about how many abuse cases went unreported for years just because people didn't want to get involved.

At least Zach Shaffer was now suspicious of Claire's story and he wouldn't hesitate to report his suspicions to the police. He wasn't afraid to get involved, Darcy thought drowsily on the edge of sleep.

Her last conscious thought was of a pair of piercing blue eyes.

The blue eyes were still in her mind when she awoke at ten o'clock the next morning. Darcy felt a perverse urge to burrow beneath the covers and think about Zach Shaffer. It had been so long since she'd had an impulse to think about any man in more than an impersonal fashion that she didn't recognize it for an instant. As soon as she did, she killed the urge by climbing out of bed and heading for the bathroom.

Standing under the hot shower spray, she remembered the heartbreaking disillusionment of her marriage and the strength it had taken to admit she'd made a mistake. Even then, it hadn't been easy to turn her back on it and embark on a college career, which she funded by working evenings as a waitress.

Allowing herself no breaks for summer vacations, she earned a degree in three grueling years, during which there was never enough money or time. She was chronically weary and behind on the rent. Yet they were satisfying years in other ways. She had taken control of her own life, had set a course and followed it to the end. She had a determined streak, she discovered, the ability to stick with a life plan through good and bad.

She'd had neither the desire nor the time for dating at college. Once she'd embarked on a career in television, she'd thrown herself into her work with the same dedication that had driven her through college in three years.

She met eligible men, of course, and there were plenty of opportunities for dates. She accepted a few of them, but the moment a man showed signs of getting serious about her, she backed off.

The problem was that they all showed the signs, sooner or later, and extricating herself became a tiresome exercise in diplomacy. Eventually, it seemed easier not to date at all, and she hadn't been out with a man socially in almost a year. It had been a conscious decision. Her life might be touched by loneliness, on occasion, but it was certainly simpler. So she banished Zach Shaffer's blue eyes from her mind.

After her shower, she started coffee brewing and put on a royal-blue shirtwaist dress. She brushed her dark hair away from her face, letting it fall naturally into bouncy, shoulder-length curls.

By two o'clock, she'd completed her errands and headed for Hope House. The middle-aged housemother, Alice Brim, greeted Darcy and ushered her into the sitting room. "Bet you came to see Claire Champlin."

"Yes. I won't disturb her if she's in a counseling session. I just wanted to check in."

"She's not here," Alice said, propping her hands on her ample, blue-jeaned hips. "She got up at eight this morning and called her husband. I tried to get her to wait till she'd talked to a counselor, but she insisted she had to let him know she was all right so he wouldn't worry." Alice grimaced as if in pain. "We both know what happened as soon as he started in on her."

Darcy sighed. "She crumbled."

Alice nodded. "He punched her guilt buttons. Said she'd put him through hell when he came home and found her gone, the kids needed her, et cetera, et cetera. He came and got her."

"She gave him the address of the shelter?" Darcy asked in consternation.

"No, I'd cautioned her about that. She met him nearly a mile from here. I did my best to keep her from making the call, Darcy."

"I'm sure you did. But there's only so much another person can do. Claire has to make her own decisions, as much as you or I would like to make them for her."

Leaving the shelter, Darcy took a meandering route to the station, trying to forget her discouragement over Claire's return home in enjoyment of the city's colorful foliage.

She was three blocks from the station when a dark-colored sedan passed her and she caught a fleeting glimpse of the driver. The sedan speeded up, whipped into a side street and disappeared.

Darcy's heart lurched with the same sickening alarm one has when escaping a head-on car collision by a hair. The driver of the sedan had looked like her ex-husband.

She fought down an irrational rush of panic. She'd seen only the man's profile and then the back of a blond head, and for a span of mere seconds. She hadn't seen him clearly enough to be sure it was Bill.

She assured herself it couldn't have been. The fleetingly glimpsed driver may have borne a passing resemblance to her ex-husband. The man's coloring and the shape of his head were similar, but that could be said of any number of men.

It could not have been Bill, she repeated to herself.

After she'd left Bill and her marriage, he'd harassed her for months, begging her to come back to him. When pleas didn't move her, he threatened to end his own life, or hers. But finally he had given up and left town. In fact, he'd moved to Nebraska, and as far as she knew he still lived there.

So forget it, she told herself—and went right on thinking about it.

Dealing with Claire Champlin last night and learning today that Claire had returned to her husband had depressed her. When she'd seen a driver who resembled Bill superficially, she'd jumped to the worst conclusion. Fear from the past had shot to the surface of her mind. But by the time she reached the station, she felt calmer. Bill was in Nebraska so she couldn't have seen him driving a car in Foleyville.

The bustle that greeted her at the station succeeded in driving out any lingering thoughts of her ex-husband. Jill Wexler, one of the station's writers and Darcy's best friend, hurried past carrying a mug of coffee. "Richard and Heather both called in sick," Jill said over her shoulder before disappearing into the office she shared with another writer.

Richard and Heather were two of the station's three field reporters. The assignments editor must be pulling out his hair about now, Darcy thought as she shrugged out of her sweater and bent to stash her purse in a desk drawer.

As she straightened, Simon, the harried assignments editor, strode into the room with a sheaf of papers in one hand and a cup of coffee in the other. Seeing Darcy, he spread his arms and proclaimed dramatically, "There is a God! My dear Darcy, you are an answer to prayers!" He slammed his cup down on Darcy's desk, sloshing coffee. "Richard and Heather had the unmitigated gall to get the flu bug at the same time."

"I heard," Darcy said, blotting the spilled coffee with a tissue.

Simon shuffled through his papers, each one containing a story idea with names of contact people and the reporter assigned to cover it. "Jeff should be here any minute." Jeff Hillman was Darcy's co-anchor. "I've been calling your place every five minutes for the past hour."

"I wasn't there."

"With my usual keen-wittedness, I finally figured that out."

"Well, I'm here now. What can I do for you?"

Simon extracted a sheet from those clutched in his hand and scanned it. "Jeff can anchor the six o'clock report alone, and we can put off a couple of these until later in the week. But I need somebody to cover this hospital story."

"Hospital?"

"County General. They're cutting the ribbon on the new pediatrics wing at five-thirty. A bunch of VIPs are supposed to put in an appearance—the governor, a couple of congressmen, the mayor..."

"You want me to cover it?"

"I hate to ask, Darcy." Jeff and Darcy rarely went into the field. The fact was that Darcy missed it sometimes.

"But you will."

"Yeah. George is down in Fayetteville on a story, and frankly I think you'd have a better chance than Jeff of getting the governor to say something interesting."

"You want me to ask him about his budget battle with the legislature?"

"If it seems appropriate."

Darcy grinned. "Since when did you worry about appropriate?"

"Well, you know how the governor is. He'll clam up if you rub him the wrong way. So apply a little feminine charm, Darcy. You know what I mean?"

Darcy eyed him askance. "I'm afraid I do, Simon."

"Knew you would." He clapped an approving hand on her shoulder. "Neither wind nor rain nor something or other..."

Darcy gave him a dry look. "I think that was said about mail carriers."

"Whatever."

She extended her hand. "Give me the assignment sheet. Who's handling the camera?"

"You can have Dee Dee. Be ready to leave at four-thirty. If the timing's right, Jeff can cut to you live during the six o'clock report. If you can get the governor to say something controversial at that moment, so much the better.''

"Like the legislature is a bunch of redneck morons?''

Simon laughed. "Yeah, like that.'' He hurried away, shuffling through his papers again and mumbling to himself.

Dee Dee, a freckled, gum-chewing bundle of pure energy, drove the van. Darcy had made a hurried search through the station's files for background material on the new hospital wing and felt adequately prepared to cover the story. Nevertheless, she was tense. Probably because she hadn't been in the field for a while, she told herself.

It had nothing to do with the fact that she was going to County General, where Zach Shaffer worked. For one thing, he might not be on duty this afternoon. For another, even if he was on duty, he'd be busy dealing with trauma cases, not standing around at the dedication ceremony. Why was she thinking about Zach Shaffer, anyway?

"You aren't coming down with the flu, too, are you?'' Dee Dee asked.

"Me? No. Do I look sick?''

Dee Dee popped her gum. "Kind of nervy. Thought you might have a headache or something.''

"I'm fine, Dee Dee.''

"Good. Can't have you getting the vapors on me, 'cause I can't operate the camera and interview the governor all at the same time. I'm quick, but not that quick.''

"I wouldn't lay any bets on it, Dee Dee."

Dee Dee grinned. "Wanta go by Smokey's for a barbecue on the way back to the station?"

"Sounds good to me."

The taping went without a hitch. The governor was in an unusually expansive mood, and after the ribbon cutting and his speech, Darcy elicited several thought-provoking comments from him about the state budget battle looming in the legislature. They got the best of these live midway through the six o'clock report. When she returned to the station, she'd put together a longer story for the ten o'clock news.

The dignitaries were leaving when Darcy glanced over the dispersing crowd of spectators and saw Zach Shaffer in a tweed jacket, white shirt and tie. He lounged against a wall, watching her.

He gave her a slow smile, and Darcy felt a maddening flush of color heat her cheeks. She nodded and turned away quickly to help Dee Dee gather up extension cords and other paraphernalia.

"How'd it go?" Darcy asked, coiling a cord into a tight circle.

"Good," Dee Dee said. "You looked great, as usual."

"How'd I sound with the governor?"

"Like you knew what you were talking about, which you did. What's wrong with you? Why are you so jumpy?"

"Hello, Darcy."

The deep voice behind her made her spin around in surprise. Zach Shaffer was smiling that lazy smile again. The fact that he'd called her Darcy and not Miss Gilbert wasn't lost on her, either.

"Oh, hello, Dr. Shaffer."

She fingered her collar, then smoothed it flat. He seemed to have unsettled her. The thought gave him a peculiar satisfaction. "I'd like to talk to you for a few minutes, if you have the time."

She looked a bit distracted. "I have to get back to the station. I came with Dee Dee here, and—"

"I can wait a few minutes, Darcy," Dee Dee put in, making Darcy want to throttle her.

"No—" Darcy began.

"I can drive you back to the station," Zach said. "I really do need to talk to you. About Claire Champlin."

Dee Dee eyed them curiously. "Go ahead, Darcy. I'll pick up a couple of barbecue beefs. Yours will be waiting when you get back."

The two of them seemed to be engaged in a silent conspiracy to leave her no graceful way to decline. Conspiracy? Don't be silly, Darcy, she chided herself. She could spare a half hour, and she did want to hear what he had to say about Claire. She shrugged philosophically. "Okay, but could we find a place to sit down?"

"The cafeteria's near here. If I can't buy you a sandwich, perhaps you'd like something to drink."

She nodded. "Tell Simon I'll be back in a half hour," she said to Dee Dee, but her eyes remained guardedly on Zach.

"This way." He indicated the direction of the cafeteria.

Darcy stepped around him and started down a hall. A light touch on her shoulder brought her up short. Darcy told herself that she imagined the electric tingling she felt through the silky material covering her shoulder.

Looking up, she saw a softening of the hard, angular face. His eyes were peculiarly gentle. She hadn't noticed that last night.

"Something wrong?"

She sucked in her breath. "Dr. Shaffer—"

"Call me Zach."

Darcy gave him a long look before she nodded abruptly. "All right . . . Zach."

Chapter 3

Zach bought two iced teas, and they found a table. "I can only stay a few minutes," Darcy said. "I have to edit tapes and write copy for the ten o'clock report. You said you wanted to talk about Claire?"

A small grin touched his mouth. She was laying down the ground rules immediately. Their conversation was to be short and to the point. But he had other ideas. "I owe you an apology."

Thrown momentarily off guard, she curled her hands around her glass and eyed him. His relaxed manner, his steady, open gaze, his friendly smile, all said that he was an honest man, not given to even small deceits. Yet he appeared to be saying he'd lured her there under false pretenses.

It wasn't the first time she'd found herself in such a predicament. Especially during the past year, when she'd made a policy of turning down dates, several men had devised clever schemes to maneuver her into accepting their company, anyway. Somehow she had expected better from Zach Shaffer, and she was disappointed.

She took a swallow of tea and set down the glass. "So...it wasn't true, when you said you wanted to talk about Claire?"

"I meant that, and I'll get to it in a moment."

"Then I don't understand."

"I'm apologizing for last night. I was short with you when I found out you hadn't reported Mrs. Champlin's husband to the police. I spoke without understanding your position as a hot line volunteer."

She remained silent while he stirred sugar into his glass.

"I was pretty stressed out. I'd been on duty ten hours when you brought her in, and we were short a nurse. Also, we'd seen a number of seriously ill and injured patients back-to-back." He set his spoon down and made a dismissive gesture with his big hands. "I'm not trying to justify my behavior. I was tired and under the gun, but I shouldn't have taken it out on you."

She met his easy smile with one of her own. It was nice to know she hadn't misjudged his honesty. "I understand. I was pretty curt, too. I thought you were playing the high-and-mighty doctor, but I see now I was wrong."

His grin was wry. "We do seem to have our share of that sort in the brotherhood." She hadn't smiled at him before, and when she did it took his breath away. He felt a reflexive tightening in the pit of his stomach. Making an effort to remain relaxed, he stretched his legs out under the table.

His knee brushed hers. Even though the contact was made through his corduroy trousers and her dress and hose, Darcy felt it like the shock of naked flesh on flesh. Her legs jerked in reflex, and she shifted them away from his.

She cleared her throat, regaining her composure. "I'm sure you have to get to work—"

"I'm not working today." He had felt the contact, too, and had detected her reaction.

"Oh. Well, I am."

"So you keep telling me." His amused expression took the sting out of the words.

"About Claire..."

"I'm discouraged about that. I made my report last night, and a police officer called me earlier this afternoon. He'd been to the Champlin house and questioned both the Champlins. Evidently you had no luck in getting her to stay away."

"She let me take her to the shelter last night, but she changed her mind early this morning and went home."

"Too bad." His long fingers caressed his glass. "It seems she's holding to her story that she fell off the porch, and her husband backs her up."

"Naturally." They exchanged ironic glances and a small silence stretched between them.

"Just before the dedication ceremony, the hospital operator paged me. Mrs. Champlin was on the phone. She was very upset with me for making the report." He drank the last of his tea. "Apparently her husband blamed her for not telling her story convincingly enough.''

She nodded in solemn understanding.

"This is the third suspected battering case I've reported," he said with a discouraged frown, "and all three women refused to file complaints against their husbands. There's nothing the police can do, and I'm getting the feeling I may be making their situations worse by making these reports."

Darcy lifted her shoulders in acknowledgement of the truth in his words. "But you will keep reporting suspicious cases, won't you?"

"I have a moral obligation," he said simply.

From someone else, it might have sounded pompous. From him, it was a mere statement of fact. "It's often the case," she said, "that these situations have to get worse before they can get better."

He sat forward and propped his elbows on the table, clasping his hands beneath his chin. "It baffles me," he said earnestly, "why these women stay with men who beat them. I know it can't be as easy to leave as it appears from the outside, but . . ." He left the sentence hanging.

Darcy schooled her expression not to show her impatience with the oft-heard remark. "No, it's very difficult. You have to understand that they're usually socially isolated. Their men see to that. They aren't allowed to have friends over, or if they are, they're afraid to risk it for fear outsiders might find out what's going on. Maybe the batterer will be drinking or in a bad mood. There's no way of predicting what might trigger a violent episode."

"That," he said quietly, "is a hell of a way to live."

"You've no idea." She spoke softly but with a conviction that didn't need volume to underline it.

He studied her thoughtfully. "But there are shelters. There's welfare. There are ways to get out if they really want to."

"That's one of the things we do on the hot line, inform them of their options. But often the financial ties aren't as binding as the emotional ones. Most battered women have threatened to leave, even tried it once or twice. Sometimes they go back because the batterer says he'll kill them or the children or himself if they don't."

He nodded slowly. "I can see why past experience would make them believe he means it." He gave her a frustrated look. "When I was talking to Claire Champlin, I sensed she felt somehow to blame for her husband's violence."

"That's common," Darcy said. "They can't give up the feeling that they're failing in some way, that if they'll just try harder to be what their men need, the beatings will stop. It's a way of maintaining the illusion that they have some control over their lives."

He leaned back in his chair, his blue eyes intent on her face. "Damned depressing volunteer work you do. I admire you for it."

She smiled fleetingly. "We have a lot of failures, but it's not all gloom and doom. As long as they're calling the hot line, there's hope. Sometimes you're able to help someone believe she can get out. Then you can direct her to a place where she'll be taken in and given support. If you're lucky, you're able to keep up their progress. If she can build some self-esteem, she can make a decent life for herself and her children. It's worth all kinds of discouragement to feel you've had a small part in the successes."

His eyes searched her face. "You're an amazing woman, Darcy," he murmured.

She looked at him almost shyly. "I'm quite ordinary, really."

She was anything but ordinary, he thought. He'd never met anyone quite like her before. "What made you choose to be a hot line volunteer?"

She saw nothing but simple curiosity in his face. But she was talking too much, feeling too relaxed. She'd better not get too comfortable, because Zach Shaffer was shrewd. Not even Darcy's closest friend, Jill Wexler, knew the painful details of her marriage. She had never talked to anyone about the abuse except the counselor she saw after leaving Bill.

Long ago, she had armed herself with a ready answer to questions like Zach's. "Almost four years ago, when I was a weekend feature reporter, I did a television series on domestic violence. Afterward, I felt I had to help in some way. In addition to working on the hot line, I occasionally speak to civic groups on the subject. I often feel frustrated that I can't do more. The general public's ignorance of the severity of the problem is appalling."

His openly admiring gaze made her study her hands. Zach Shaffer was a rare man, one whom she felt attracted to. He made her feel as though she could talk to him for hours about anything. He put her at ease, as though he were an old friend. But he wasn't an old friend, she reminded herself. He was a virtual stranger, a much too attractive one.

When she moved her head, soft, dark curls slid over her shoulder. Zach wondered how it would feel to bury his face in her hair, to fill his lungs with its clean, sweet scent, to feel its silken strands sliding through his fingers.

She was unaware of his intention until he'd reached out his big hand and his fingers tucked an errant wisp of hair behind her ear. "Darcy—"

She stared at him, her eyes guarded. Only the tight linking of her hands on the table revealed an inner tension.

"Are you involved with anyone?" he asked quietly. His fingers lingered for the space of several heartbeats, then brushed her cheek as his hand dropped away.

She dropped her hands out of sight beneath the table and schooled her expression to reveal nothing. "Why do you ask?"

Though on the surface she knew she appeared distant and uninvolved, she felt a curious mixture of wariness and an odd sense of longing for something that could not be.

He smiled, a gentle smile that softened the firm line of his mouth. "That should be obvious. I want to know you better. I'd like to ask you out."

"No, don't do that." Her small laugh was strained. "I can't go out with you, Zach." How strange that she should feel that little flicker of regret. She collected her scattered thoughts and pushed back her chair. "Now, I really must get back to the station. Thanks for the tea." She kept her gaze steady on his face and even managed an ingenuous look.

As she stepped around the table, he rose to his feet, his long length unfolding with easy grace for such a large man. "I'm driving you, remember?"

She felt foolish because she *had* forgotten. "I can't let you go to the trouble. I'll grab a cab." She smiled to soften the refusal. "The station will pay for it. Goodbye, Zach."

His hand brushed her shoulder as she turned away, a light caress that felt as intimate as a passionate kiss.

"Goodbye, Darcy," Zach echoed softly. He watched her cross the cafeteria and stride quickly out the door. She had turned him down flat but, perversely, he was more intrigued by her than ever. He was far from ready to give up his quest to know what, besides compassion for battered women, was behind her beautiful, successful, articulate facade.

Darcy was too busy for the next few hours to give Zach Shaffer much thought. She ate her barbecue beef sandwich with a can of cola from a machine while working with Jill on her script for the ten o'clock report.

After an hour, they took a coffee break in the women's lounge. Jill wanted to talk about the coming weekend, which she planned to enjoy with her boyfriend, Charles, at his parents' lake cabin.

"You're spending a lot of time with Charles these days," Darcy observed.

"All the time I can," Jill admitted. "I'm crazy about him, Darcy."

Darcy smiled at the excited sparkle in Jill's eyes when she spoke of Charles. In a detached sort of way, she was glad for her friend's happiness. She felt no envy or desire for someone like Charles in her own life. Getting out of a destructive relationship was so much harder than getting into it in the first place. And how could you ever be sure what the relationship would be like until you were enmeshed in it? She'd been blind to Bill's violent tendencies until after they were married.

"That's nice," she murmured.

Jill laughed. "But you wouldn't want to be in my place."

Darcy shrugged good-naturedly. "Charles is a fine fellow, but—"

"Charles has nothing to do with it," Jill cut in, "although even you must admit he's cute and sweet and going places at the brokerage house."

Darcy nodded in acknowledgment of Jill's assessment.

"I've known you for three years," Jill went on, "and I've yet to see you lose your head over a man. Sometimes I think you don't even like them."

"I like them well enough," Darcy protested mildly.

"As long as they keep their distance?" In the past, Jill had tried to arrange dates for Darcy. Fortunately she had given up on that long ago.

"I don't have time for a love affair, Jill. There are only so many hours in the day."

"You're the most single-minded woman I know, Darcy. I know your marriage didn't last long, but I've often wondered how you ever had time to get married in the first place."

"I was very young," Darcy said lightly, "and I didn't know what I wanted to be when I grew up." She could not envision herself ever marrying again. Darcy had an almost phobic fear of giving up her hard-won control in any area of her life. There were, she admitted, times when she felt lonely and even longed for a man's closeness on a short-term basis. When that happened, all she had to do was compare her married life with her life at present, and the feelings always passed. Life was full of trade-offs, she told herself.

Jill studied her gravely for an instant. "It doesn't have to be an either-or situation. No man worth his salt will ask you to give up your career for him. I know I don't plan to give up mine if Charles and I eventually get married. I want to have it all."

"I already have everything I want," Darcy said. She stood and tossed her empty Styrofoam cup in the wastebasket. "If I want to keep it, I'd better get back to work."

Although she usually looked forward to the weekend as a time to rest and recharge her energy batteries for the coming week, Darcy took home enough work Friday night to keep her busy all day Saturday. It occurred to her that her need to keep her mind occupied was in some way connected to Zach Shaffer, but she banished the thought immediately.

About noon, Darcy made a quick trip to the library for background material on a story she was preparing. Other than that, she stayed inside, buried in work. Even the telephone cooperated and made not a sound all day.

At ten-thirty that night, when the phone finally did ring, Darcy had just risen from her desk, stretched tiredly and headed for the kitchen and a snack. The ringing sounded unnaturally loud in the quiet apartment.

Combing her fingers through her hair, Darcy reached for the receiver.

"Darcy, I hope I didn't wake you." Darcy recognized Claire Champlin's voice immediately.

"You didn't. I've been working all day, and it's nice to hear a human voice."

"I wouldn't have called if I didn't really need to talk. I won't make a habit of calling you at home, I promise."

"Claire, I said it was all right." Claire didn't reply immediately, and Darcy realized she was trying to compose herself or perhaps work up her nerve for what she'd called to say. "I went to the shelter to check on you Friday afternoon, but they said you'd gone home."

"A policeman came to see us," Claire said haltingly.

"I heard about that."

"The doctor who set my arm reported it. I didn't tell the police anything, but Ralph was furious. He started drinking and went to work with a six-pack of beer. The only reason he hasn't been fired before now is that he can fix any machine made. He doubles as a repairman between security patrols." She sighed wistfully before returning to the crux of her problem. "He ranted and raved all day, got himself all worked up again."

"Did he beat you?"

Claire made a sniffling sound. "Yes," she whispered. "Thank goodness the kids weren't here. They're with my mother this weekend."

"Are you all right?"

"Nothing's broken, but my shoulders and chest are black-and-blue." She gulped loudly. "I don't know what to do, Darcy."

"I think you do," Darcy said quietly. "We've discussed the alternatives before."

Claire drew in a deep breath and let it out slowly. "He's not going to change, is he?"

"Based on your past experience, what do you think?"

The question required no answer. "I think I'd like to go back to the shelter. Could you take me?"

"Are you going to call Ralph in the morning and let him talk you into coming home?"

"No, I won't call him."

"I'll be glad to come and get you, Claire, but you have to promise me you'll really try to stay at least a week and get involved in group counseling sessions."

Claire said nothing for a long moment, and Darcy knew how hard it was for her to make such a promise. She could remember feeling utterly helpless and terrified when she was agonizing over whether to leave Bill. Decisions were so difficult in those days.

"I don't know..."

"The housemother and the counselors at Hope House will help you," Darcy said. "You don't have to go through this alone."

"All right," Claire said at last. "If my mother can keep the kids, I'll stay a week."

"Good. Pack a suitcase. I'll be there as soon as I can."

"Darcy," a secretary called, "there's a Dr. Shaffer on the line for you." She put her hand over the phone and added in a stage whisper, "He has a sexy voice!"

Overhearing, Dee Dee gave Darcy a mischievous grin and said, "If you don't want him, give him my phone number."

"I may just do that," Darcy retorted as she picked up the phone on her desk. "Darcy Gilbert speaking."

"Darcy, this is Zach. Can you talk?"

"For a minute." She sat down and, kicking off her shoes, leaned back in her chair. The story conference had lasted nearly two hours, and she'd had to argue hard for two stories she particularly wanted to do. She'd won, but she felt drained. "Actually, I'm glad to have a chance to tell you Claire Champlin went back to the shelter Saturday night. She agreed to stay a while, and so far she's holding to it."

Zach noted the businesslike note in her voice, but hadn't there been a little hint of interest when she first came on the line? "I'm glad to hear that. I've thought a lot about her problems the past few days."

"I'll tell her you're concerned about her," Darcy said with a small smile. She was sure Zach hadn't called to talk about Claire Champlin's problems. "I know she'll appreciate it."

"I'm ashamed to admit how little I know about the causes and cures of domestic violence. It wasn't one of the subjects we covered in med school, and it occurred to me that health-care professionals in general aren't well educated on the subject.''

Still suspicious that all this was just a roundabout route leading to the real reason for this call, Darcy remained alert for him to switch conversational tracks on her. At the same time, she found herself listening to the deep, male voice and enjoying it. She found herself remembering his eyes and the gentleness with which he'd touched her hair. A disturbing tingle worked its way down her spine.

"Darcy, are you still there?"

She shook herself from the seduction of dangerous thoughts. "Still here."

"All that was by way of explaining that I've had a brainstorm. I'd like to talk to you about it over lunch."

For a split second, she entertained a traitorous thought. Why should she say no to a simple luncheon invitation? But she hesitated only for a second, and then she remembered that it wouldn't remain simple. It never had in the past. Normal men wanted more from a woman than an occasional lunch. And Zach was certainly a normal man.

It was with an unfamiliar twinge of regret that she said, "Zach, I told you the other day that I won't go out with you."

"I heard you," he said smoothly, "loud and clear. But I assumed you meant going out as in date. I admit it bruised my ego a bit, but I recovered. This is strictly business."

"Hmm." Zach Shaffer was too clever and too charming. Honest he may be, but in this instance she didn't quite trust him. "Then," she said briskly, "I don't see why we can't discuss it on the telephone."

"It's too long and involved," Zach said just as briskly, as though he'd been prepared for this ploy. "I assume you have work to do there."

She almost chuckled. He wasn't easily deflected. One might even say he was stubborn. "Piles of it."

"What time do you go to work?"

"I don't think that—"

"Never mind. The secretary told me you usually come in about three."

"She *what*? She had no right to do that."

"Don't blame her. I sort of wormed it out of her."

Darcy could easily imagine Zach turning on the sweetness and charm and the secretary promptly melting like butter left out of the refrigerator on a summer day. "She's paid not to let people worm things out of her."

"Give her a break, Darcy," Zach said in a deep, coaxing tone of voice.

"Oh, all right. It's no big deal. Now, what is this business you wish to discuss?"

"I want you, as a representative of the domestic violence hot line, to speak to the trauma center personnel."

"We don't have to go to lunch to settle that. Of course I'll do it."

Zach heaved a sigh. "If only it were that simple. I have to clear it with administration. In order to make my case, I need to know what you'll cover, point by point.''

Darcy scowled at the telephone dial. Naturally, she didn't have time to go into all that now. She had a strong suspicion Zach had counted on it. She hesitated another moment before asking, "When do you want to meet?" He had made her an offer she couldn't refuse, and he damn well knew it.

"Is tomorrow at one okay with you? We can go to the French Hen. It's not far from the TV station." He sounded satisfied with himself.

"Tomorrow's fine."

"I'll pick you up. Give me your address."

"No," Darcy said quickly, "I'll need my car. I'll meet you at the restaurant."

"Whatever you say," he replied good-naturedly. "One o'clock at the restaurant."

Darcy said goodbye and hung up, turning to see Jill and Dee Dee near the coffee machine, heads together. They'd been watching her, and both grinned unabashedly when she caught them at it. Obviously Dee Dee had been telling Jill about Zach.

"So he's taking you to lunch," Jill observed.

"Eavesdroppers," Darcy accused.

Dee Dee shrugged matter-of-factly. "We couldn't help overhearing."

"Gee, why didn't you tell me you can't resist redheads?" Jill said. "If I'd known, I'd have found you one long ago."

"The color of Dr. Shaffer's hair is irrelevant. This is business," Darcy snapped and turned away, cursing the heat that flushed her cheeks.

Dear heaven, what was wrong with her? She'd been fending off would-be suitors for years, and on occasion she'd had to do it at the station within sight and sound of her co-workers. At one point, her co-anchor Jeff Hillman had been very persistent in trying to break down her resolve. She'd been more persistent in her determination not to let him.

Turning down Jeff had never flustered her. Nor was she in the habit of blushing like a backward teenager. Zach elicited emotions in her that were foreign, and quite inexplicable.

Chapter 4

The French Hen was a small restaurant, tucked away on a narrow side street. It was a popular lunch spot for people who worked downtown, owing its popularity as much to the relaxed atmosphere and strolling violinists as to its menu, which ran to soups, salads, sandwiches and a variety of crepe dishes.

Zach was already seated at a table when Darcy arrived at ten after one. He smiled and rose as she approached, going around the table to hold her chair.

"Sorry I'm late," Darcy said breathlessly. "I got hung up in traffic."

Zach watched her pluck her napkin from beside her plate and smooth it over her lap. She looked stunning in a hot pink silk shirt. Several gold chains glittered in the vee created by the shirt's open collar, and there were small gold hoops at her ears. Each time he saw her face-to-face, he was surprised anew by her beauty, having convinced himself that she couldn't possibly be as lovely as he remembered.

"No problem. My shift doesn't start until three. And we've missed most of the lunch crowd, so we shouldn't be bothered by people eyeing our table with longing."

She nodded and reached for a menu. She glanced over it perfunctorily, then laid it aside. "I'll have the vegetarian sandwich on a croissant and decaffeinated coffee."

After giving their order to the waitress, he asked, "Are you a vegetarian?"

She smiled. "Only on my disciplined days. I'll go along for two or three weeks, eating virtuously and feeling smug about it, and then a desperate craving for a thick, juicy steak or some barbecue hits me." She fingered the gold chains idly. "At which point, I fall off the wagon. I suppose that means I have a weak streak in my character."

He chuckled. "A good thing. You'd be insufferable if you were as flawless as you look."

"The right hairdresser and makeup can do wonders," she said dismissingly.

"While the male of the species has to struggle along with what God gave him."

She eyed him with faint amusement. "Fishing for compliments, Dr. Shaffer?"

"And if I am?"

"You do very well with what God gave you, as I'm sure you know."

More than very well, she added silently. His blue cable-stitched sweater accentuated the color of his eyes—they looked almost too blue to be believed. The hazy, Indian-summer sunlight pouring through a bank of windows struck coppery highlights in his hair and emphasized the gold tips on his long lashes; the angle at which it fell created faint shadows in the hollows of his lean cheeks and the cleft in his chin, making his face look as though it was chiseled from stone, the angles honed and clean.

He looked at her curiously. "Do you think so? That's encouraging."

She lifted a brow. "It wasn't meant as encouragement. I was merely stating the obvious."

"Better watch yourself," he teased. "That almost sounded like a compliment."

She looked away from him, flicking a glance over a violinist playing a sultry love song for a young couple seated across the room. Restlessly, she touched her throat. She felt his eyes on her. As their waitress set their sandwiches and drinks in front of them, Darcy ran her fingers over the cold, gleaming steel of her dinner knife.

"Thank you," Zach said to the waitress, though his gaze never left Darcy. As the waitress walked away, he imprisoned Darcy's restless fingers in his big hand. "I know you want me to *think* you aren't encouraging me. But I keep getting these subtle signals from you... Maybe they're unconscious."

She sat very still as his hand tightened around hers and his thumb caressed the tiny pulse beating on the inside of her wrist. The simple action felt so intimate it took all of Darcy's will to meet his gaze without looking away again.

Was she sending out unintended signals? She couldn't deny that she felt inexplicably drawn to him, that his closeness unsettled her and his touch made her feel panic and an impulse to bolt before something disastrous happened. She could not discern the shape of the feared disaster, but somehow she knew it was real. Because it was, she said with more force than was necessary, "That's ridiculous."

"Is it?" he asked in a soft, reflective voice. "Then why do I make you so nervous?"

"I'm not nervous!"

His thumb insinuated itself beneath the wristband of her shirt, sending warmth tingling up her arm. "You keep fidgeting with your neck chains and the silverware," he pointed out. "I've never seen you do that on television. You're as cool as a cucumber in front of the camera."

She felt anything but cool at the moment. She wanted to pull away from his touch but feared it would only confirm what he already suspected, that she found him attractive. But something more kept her immobile. His long, strong fingers on her skin, the gentle caressing movement, produced erotic sensations that she hadn't felt in so long—she couldn't even remember how long—perhaps she'd never felt this seductive, mesmerizing warmth that was stealing through her body, paralyzing her.

She caught herself wanting to turn her hand over, lace her fingers through his and cling to him. Her weakness frightened her. Sucking in a deep breath, she drew her hand from his. "You're very good at seduction, Doctor," she murmured, "but what is the point—"

Zach was not deflected. "I'm still thinking about how cool you are on camera. Maybe *that's* the point," he said slowly, as though the insight took shape as he spoke. "The camera's between you and the world. It lets you stay at a distance." But she hadn't stayed at a distance just now. He'd felt the erratic leap of her pulse beneath his thumb, the heating of her skin where he touched her.

He wished they were in a less public place. Yet he hadn't meant to take her hand like that in the first place. It had happened almost before he knew it. He had planned to play this more cautiously, but she'd caught him off guard simply by walking into the restaurant and reminding him how desirable she was.

Now that he was no longer touching her, she could recover her detachment. "Are you taking up psychiatry?" she asked with a faint touch of disdain.

It was warranted, he admitted. His comment had been too simplistic, like something in a pop-psychology magazine. She was a very complicated woman, that much he knew by now. Whatever stood between them wasn't inconsequential. It went very deep.

He guessed there was no other man in her life at present. Maybe a man in her past had broken her heart, and she'd never recovered from it, though he'd have found it easier to believe the reverse. Or maybe he reminded her of someone she didn't want to remember.

"I deserved that," he said. "I'm sorry."

She looked at him levelly for a long moment, then with a small nod she accepted his apology. She picked up her sandwich and bit into it, saying nothing more until she'd eaten half of it. Then, "Shall we get to the point of this meeting?"

His hand tightened involuntarily on his napkin as he brought it to his mouth. "Give me a thumbnail sketch of what you'd cover in your speech."

"All right," Darcy agreed, sorry about the bleak disappointment in his eyes but unwilling to take back anything she'd said. "I start by shattering some of the myths surrounding battered women—that they're very few in number, that they're found only among the poor or minority groups, that they're uneducated or crazy or masochistic."

He looked faintly abashed. "I confess I've been guilty of believing some of that. Go on."

"I cover some of the characteristics they do have in common, such as low self-esteem, and some of the coercive techniques used by batterers. Finally, I'll talk about the hot line and the women's shelter, Hope House. I'll stress the need for more effective laws to protect these women, more shelters and counseling facilities."

She had spoken with great earnestness and no trace of the nervousness she showed when he tried to find out more about her personally. He'd known other women who were consumed by a cause and had found them tiresome after a while because they saw everything and everyone in the light of that cause. In time, he came to view them as preachy and asexual.

But Darcy didn't fit the pattern. She was an intelligent, compassionate, strikingly attractive, totally feminine woman with an honesty and directness that disarmed him. Already, after a few brief encounters, he felt drawn to her as he had been to no other woman. It was as though he'd been captured by an enchanter's spell. And he wasn't struggling very hard to break free, he admitted ruefully. Instead, he wanted to go deeper, to peel away the layers and solve the mystery that was Darcy Gilbert.

"That helps me. I'll use it when I talk to the administrator tomorrow."

In pleading her cause, she had forgotten to be guarded. He gazed into her intent, clear eyes and felt as if he could see down to her soul. But he knew he couldn't, not all the way down. She always held something back.

"I don't think I can be as convincing as you, but I'll do my best."

"I'll be glad to talk to him personally, if you think it'll help."

"I may take you up on that, but let me try first."

The violinist paused at their table and began playing another slow love song. He was middle-aged and paunchy, but he became a romantic figure when he coaxed beautiful music from his violin. He smiled at them benignly, obviously assuming they were lovers.

A warm flush of discomfort suffused Darcy's body. While the music lasted, she stared at her hands, linked primly on the tablecloth. The music was romantic, but plaintive and melancholy at the same time. It spawned an unexpected sadness in her. She was glad when the violinist moved on to another table.

When she looked up, Zach was watching her. She threw off the sadness of the music and tilted her head. "Tell me about your work. Do you always have the late shift?"

"No, the three shifts are rotated among three three-man teams of trauma center physicians. We work days for two weeks, then evenings for two and so on. I was on three to eleven when you brought Mrs. Champlin in, but I'd agreed to cover the first half of the next shift for a friend who was laid up with a virus. Another doctor took the second half of his shift."

"You like your work." It wasn't a question.

He nodded. "I never wanted to be anything but a doctor. When I did my rotation in the emergency room during my residency, I knew immediately that trauma medicine was my niche. It's real hands-on medicine, life and death stuff. I know that sounds melodramatic, but that's how I felt. Still do."

She looked down, seeing his hands lying on the table inches from hers. His hands were square and large, strong-looking hands, but she knew they could be incredibly gentle, too, as they'd been when he touched her in the hospital cafeteria. She was sure that, with a mere touch, he could make a sick person feel comforted. His fingers were long and blunt, dusted with red-brown hair. Her hands looked pale and absurdly small by comparison.

She raised her eyes to meet his. "I felt something similar when I first walked into a television studio. The air crackled with tension and excitement, as if what was going on there really mattered."

For an instant, their gazes locked and a subtle connection was made. They had revealed something of themselves to each other, something important, and they had inched closer as a result.

Darcy dragged her glance away first. Her fingers fluttered to her throat again. "I'd better go to work."

Moments later, they stood on the sidewalk in front of the restaurant. "I'm pleased about the possibility of your speaking to our personnel," Zach said.

"So am I, and I meant what I said about talking to the administrator myself."

A gust of wind eddied around the corner and down the tunnel created by tall buildings on either side of the street. It whipped Darcy's hair into her face. Zach reached out and gathered a handful of dark strands, holding it out of her eyes. His other hand came up to frame her face.

Darcy felt his long fingers tunneling through her hair. For an endless pause in time, while his palms smoothed over her head in the oddly gentling way in which she imagined he might console a sick child, she stood very still, hardly breathing.

"Thanks for lunch," she murmured.

Bending down, he brushed his lips across her forehead so lightly it was like a breath or a whisper.

"The pleasure was mine. I'll be in touch."

"Goodbye." Still unmoving, she watched him walk away from her, hands thrust deep into his trousers pockets. Momentarily, she came to her senses and walked in the opposite direction, head bowed against the wind.

Darcy's mind drifted to that moment on the sidewalk several times that afternoon and evening. The memory remained so vivid that, when she called it back, she could see the corner of Zach's mouth lift in a lazy grin and crinkling of the skin at the corners of his eyes. She could feel the gentle smoothing of his hands on her hair and the warm, soft brush of his mouth on her brow. She could even hear the mournful moan of the wind. Odd how some moments in life remained so real in memory.

And she was only etching that moment with Zach ever deeper in her mind by thinking of it repeatedly, she reminded herself with chagrin.

Wednesday morning glowed with the golden haze of another Indian summer day. Darcy slept late and awoke to feel the sun's gentle warmth on her face. She lay for a while, gazing out her bedroom window at the deep red leaves of a maple tree against a soft blue sky. It was too lovely a day, she decided, to stay indoors. After her shower, she'd have a leisurely cup or two of coffee with her paper in the enclosed courtyard shared by the six ground-floor apartments in the building.

Later, she remembered the bakery not far from the television station with its sidewalk tables and decided to have lunch there before going to work.

Her mellow mood stayed with her as she ambled from the station's parking lot, where she left her car, to the bakery four blocks away, hands tucked in the pockets of her green-and-wine plaid dress. She had tied the sleeves of a green cotton cardigan around her shoulders, in case the air felt nippy, but she wasn't going to need it, after all. When she reached the bakery, she draped the sweater over the back of her chair and ordered spinach quiche and a fruit cup.

She pulled a half-finished novel from her purse and settled down to read while she waited for her meal. Soon she was lost in a fictional world.

"Darcy! Hi."

The voice behind her was so unexpected that she jumped and the book flew from her hand and fell to the sidewalk.

"Here, I'll get that. Sorry I startled you."

He scooped up the book and handed it to her. Then, almost in the same movement, he slid into a chair beside her. She stared at him in stunned silence. It could only have been the particular set of circumstances in which she found herself that had kept her from recognizing him in that first instant. She had been floating on a lazy cloud of well-being ever since she awoke that morning. Further, she'd been deep in her novel when he spoke to her. There were physical differences, too. His blond hair was clipped much shorter than she remembered, and he no longer had a moustache.

Acceptance overcame denial just as the waitress arrived with her lunch. He ordered coffee, then leaned back in his chair and smiled at her. The smile that had once made her feel weak and sappy now made her feel sick. Without any real evidence, she was convinced he'd been waiting for her outside the station when she'd left her car. He'd followed her to the café.

Suddenly she remembered that glimpse of a man's profile in a passing car, the one she'd convinced herself wasn't Bill. But it had been, and she knew somehow that he'd seen her then, too. Perhaps he'd even been driving around looking for her, since she didn't see how he could know where she lived now. She had taken pains to keep her address from becoming public knowledge.

"You're a long way from Nebraska, Bill." Her lips felt stiff, cold. She put on her sweater against the sudden chill in the air, then clasped her hands in her lap to still their distressing tendency to tremble.

"I'm working in Foleyville again. I moved back a couple of weeks ago." He sipped his coffee, eyeing her over the rim of the mug. Like a tomcat waiting to pounce, Darcy thought, and knew that she was probably being paranoid. He set his mug down. "You'd better eat that quiche before it gets cold."

Darcy swallowed to wet her dry mouth. Stirring, she picked up her fork and began to eat. The spinach quiche, her favorite item on the bakery's menu, tasted like cardboard.

"You look great, Darcy. Really great."

"You look well yourself," she said grudgingly. Why was she sitting here and carrying on this stupid, polite conversation with her ex-husband when what she wanted to do was run away as fast as she could?

She kept her gaze lowered and forced another bite of quiche down her throat. Why? Because she was her own person now, and he couldn't hurt her anymore. Because she had ordered lunch and she would darn well eat it. Because she had to show him that she'd put

him and the marriage behind her, that he no longer
had the power to intimidate her.

"I was in therapy for two years," he announced, as
though he expected a medal.

She looked up. His hazel eyes were earnest, guile-
less. But she didn't trust him. Perhaps he'd been in
therapy and perhaps not. Anyway, it didn't matter. He
had nothing to do with her anymore. If she'd had the
power, she would have wiped all memory of him and
the marriage from her brain.

He obviously expected a comment from her, but she
didn't know what to say. Remembering how she used
to chatter endlessly, trying to divert him when he lost
his temper, she kept her mouth firmly closed.

"I'm glad I ran into you because there are some
things I need to say to you."

"It's not necessary." She put down her fork and
fumbled for her purse and book. She was no longer
hungry. And she didn't want to hear an apology. She'd
heard too many when they were married, and they
never meant anything.

"Yes, it is. I know I was a miserable s.o.b. There's
no excuse for the way I treated you, and I'm really
sorry, Darcy. I don't expect you to forgive me easily. I
just wanted you to know I got help and I've already
joined an Abusers Anonymous group here, not that I
really need the support anymore. I know how to deal
with my temper now. I'm a different man."

Darcy pushed back her chair. "If you feel better
about yourself, that's good." She stood abruptly and
he scrambled to his feet.

"Darcy, wait—"

"I have to go to work."

"I thought—maybe—I mean, could I see you now and then? We could go to a movie or something."

"No," she said sharply. Dear God, could he really believe she'd consider beginning another relationship with him? She couldn't even look at him without feeling nauseated. Nothing would be gained by trying to frame a diplomatic refusal. Bill didn't understand diplomacy. "I don't want you in my life, Bill. Don't try to see me again."

She knew she'd made him angry by the way his lips thinned and the skin around his mouth paled. When she was married to him, that look had been the signal for her to start chattering. By the time of their final months together, she'd learned he would turn whatever she said into an insult, an excuse for his accelerating temper. So she'd begun to tiptoe around him and remain silent when he got upset. That seemed to enrage him even more. In counseling, she'd learned that it had never mattered what she said, or how much, because she wasn't responsible for his anger. She was merely a convenient target.

Clutching her purse to her breast, she walked away from him as fast as she could without actually succumbing to her panicky impulse to run. Her heart beat loudly in her ears, and she swallowed the sharp taste of acid. She was trembling.

Only when she'd turned a corner and knew he could no longer see her did she slow down and attempt to calm herself. It doesn't matter, she told herself. He can't hurt you anymore.

Foleyville was a good-sized city. Their paths weren't likely to cross often. He'd moved back to town, but nothing else had changed.

She had to forget about him. She couldn't go around searching the faces of drivers in passing cars or looking over her shoulder every time she walked on the street. The meeting could have been accidental. There was nothing to indicate he'd followed her to the bakery except her own baseless conviction. He'd said nothing, done nothing that was even remotely threatening. She'd *felt* threatened, but that was all in her mind. She had control of her own life now, and she could not let irrational fears affect her.

As soon as she reached the station, she went to the receptionist and the two secretaries and cautioned them not to give her unlisted home phone number or address to anyone. She was merely restating a station policy, but she felt better for doing it.

Although the three women looked at her curiously, she gave no explanation for her sudden concern. A few minutes later, when she glanced in a mirror and saw her ashen face, she realized the women had been curious about her pinched expression, not what she'd said.

She plunged into work. By the time she had to go on the air at six o'clock, she was outwardly composed. Only Darcy was aware of the faint trembling of her hands, which she kept out of view of the camera as much as possible. Her voice was clear and firm, and she missed no cues.

When they were off the air, the producer said, "Good job, kids. By the way, Jeff, that foliage tour follows the Talimena Drive, not Talihena."

"I knew it the minute I said it," Jeff said. "Sorry."

Only half hearing, Darcy slumped in her chair, realizing for the first time that her body, beneath her plaid dress, was bathed with a film of perspiration. Her impeccable performance on camera had required an enormous effort of will because, all the time, she'd been wondering, Is Bill watching the broadcast? Stop this, she ordered herself.

"You okay, Darcy?"

She glanced at her co-anchor and managed a smile. "I'm fine, Jeff. Just thinking about expanding that day-care center story a little for the ten o'clock report. Can we give it another thirty seconds, Rance?"

The producer nodded. "We can take it out of the commission hearing spot. That ran too long."

"I'll get to work on it," Darcy said.

She was revising the story when Jill stopped at her desk a while later. "The receptionist said you looked upset when you came to work."

Darcy finished the sentence she was writing before she glanced up. "She's scraping the bottom of the barrel for things to talk about, I guess. My stomach was a little queasy, but I'm over it now."

"All work and no play, Darcy."

"I think I've heard this tape before," Darcy said, turning back to the day-care story.

Jill sighed. "I worry about you."

"Well, don't," Darcy replied curtly.

"You have no social life, no fun," Jill went on unrelentingly. "The only thing you seem interested in besides work is that hot line, which is about the most emotionally draining thing I can think of. It's unnatural, and it's beginning to show. You were strung as tight as a drum on the six o'clock show."

Darcy's head shot up. "Did Rance say something?"

Jill shook her head. "I know you better than the others. I don't think anyone else noticed. But, Darcy, you're obviously under a lot of stress. If you don't learn to lighten up, you're heading for trouble."

"I'm okay, really." Just then the telephone rang, and Darcy nearly jumped out of her chair. Jill shot her a speaking glance as Darcy pulled her gaze from the telephone on her desk. A secretary would answer it.

"Why don't you go to the lake with Charles and me Saturday? We're going up just for the day."

Darcy smiled. "Charles would love that."

"He wouldn't mind. He likes you. You and I could go for a long walk while he's fishing. Think about it, will you?"

"Sure," Darcy said to get Jill off the subject for the moment. She had no intention of intruding into their weekend.

The producer's secretary thrust her head out of her office. "Phone call for you, Darcy. It's Zach Shaffer."

Until that moment, Darcy hadn't realized how rigidly alert she'd been ever since the first ring of the telephone. Or that, subconsciously, she'd been half convinced it was Bill on the other end of the line. It was a relief to learn it was Zach. She reached for the receiver almost gratefully.

"Hello, Zach." She was aware of Jill, still hovering beside the desk.

"Hi. Are you busy?"

"Moderately so. How did your meeting with the administrator go?"

"I didn't get a final decision. He agreed to think about it, but frankly he's not very supportive of the idea."

Darcy picked up her pen and doodled on a scratch pad. She turned half away from Jill. "Why?" she asked. "If it's money, I'll speak for nothing."

"It's not the money. He's afraid we're going to open a whole can of worms, make the employees overly suspicious so they'll be filing a report on every other woman we see. He doesn't believe there are many battering victims in Foleyville. Apparently he thinks we're living in a Norman Rockwell painting. He says the media blow up isolated cases for shock value."

The administrator's reaction was not unexpected, but it still made Darcy feel frustrated and indignant. "I'm not an alarmist." She drew a stick-figure man on the scratch pad, then scribbled it out. "Darn it, I wish I could talk to him myself. I think I could convince him of the need for educating his employees on the subject."

"Actually, that's why I called." She thought she detected a smile in Zach's voice. "There's an employee awards banquet Saturday night. Go to the banquet with me, and I'll make sure you get a few minutes to talk to him alone."

If he was smiling, no wonder, Darcy thought. She'd played right into his hands. She dropped the pen and flexed her fingers, easing the tightness caused by clutching the pen too hard. "Don't you think a meeting in his office would be more appropriate?"

"He'll be in a sociable mood Saturday night, and he won't be expecting to see you. I think you'd have better luck then."

Darcy suppressed a smile. "Did anyone ever tell you you're devious?"

"Whiteley won't hold it against you."

"That isn't what I meant."

"You think I'm using this to get you to go out with me? Why, Ms. Gilbert, I'm wounded."

Darcy laughed at the fake humility in his tone. "No, you aren't."

He chuckled. "I promise to behave properly—unless, by some wild twist of fortune, you prefer a little impropriety."

Darcy leaned back in her chair, catching Jill's approving smile. She looked away, but she found herself wanting to accept Zach's invitation. Being allowed to speak to the trauma center employees was important to her. She wanted the opportunity to convince the hospital administrator that it was needed. Beyond that, some of what Jill had said to her had hit home. Her overreaction to seeing her ex-husband again proved that she wasn't handling stress too well these days. Perhaps a change of scene would help. "I'll let you know what I prefer, never fear."

"I'm sure," he said a bit ruefully. "Does that mean you accept?"

"I'll go to the banquet with you, Zach," she said and added pointedly, "in order to talk to the administrator."

"Duly noted."

"Is it formal?"

"Semi. The happy hour starts at 6:30. That will be the best time to talk to Whiteley. I'll pick you up at 6:15."

She gave him her address. After replacing the receiver, she said, "Stop beaming like the mother of the bride, Jill. It's business."

"Of course," said Jill. "I conduct all *my* business at formal banquets."

"Semiformal," Darcy corrected. She picked up her pen and resumed work on the script. After a moment, Jill let her be and went to her own desk, clearly assuming Darcy was once again deep in the day-care story.

How could Jill know it was several minutes before Darcy could concentrate on the story or anything else except the panicky little thrill she felt when it finally dawned on her that whatever she called it, date or business, Saturday night's banquet was a social occasion. She was going to get dressed up, and Zach was going to call for her and return her to her apartment when the evening was over.

Darcy, she told herself, if it looks like a date and feels like a date, it might very well *be* a date.

Chapter 5

The hospital administrator, Frank Whiteley, was a distinguished-looking man in his middle fifties. His silver hair added to the impression of experienced wisdom, and his superbly tailored dinner jacket almost camouflaged the excess weight he carried around his midsection.

At the moment, he was standing in a small alcove at one end of an anteroom off the country club's large banquet hall. He was engaged in conversation with a younger man, whom Zach identified as Dan Leonard, an internal medicine specialist on staff at County.

"I'll introduce you," Zach said softly near Darcy's ear as he placed a hand against the small of her back to steer her toward the alcove. "Then I'll try to draw Dan aside and leave the two of you alone."

Darcy reminded herself that this was the moment she'd anticipated, her sole reason for accepting Zach's invitation. She'd almost forgotten it amid the flurry of introductions, the swirl and glitter of the silk, satin and lace adorning the women and the men's black and white dinner jackets.

After careful consideration of her rather extensive wardrobe, Darcy had worn a long, gold lamé jacket over a pencil-slim black, backless dress. Five minutes before Zach arrived, she began to wonder if she should have chosen something a little less dramatic, less partyish. But it was too late to change.

When she saw Zach's black trousers and white dinner jacket, she felt secure in her choice. They couldn't have looked better together if they'd consulted each other about their wardrobe, she admitted, noting the gleam of approval in Zach's eyes. He really was an extremely attractive man. Not that Zach's attraction was the point of this outing, she reminded herself. It was, in fact, very much beside the point.

Dr. Leonard looked around as Zach and Darcy approached. His eyes flew to Darcy, widened slightly in recognition, then narrowed in interested speculation. "Hello, Zach. Your taste in women has moved up several notches. Or maybe Lady Luck's decided to smile on you."

Zach clapped a hand on Leonard's shoulder. "Couldn't get a date for the evening? Tough, old man." Before Leonard could respond, Zach introduced Darcy to the two men. "Frank's the man holding the hospital purse strings, so be nice to him, Darcy. And watch out for Dan. He fancies himself a ladies' man."

Dan Leonard's deep suntan had to come from a sunlamp, Darcy thought. His smile exposed perfect white teeth. He was handsome enough to be a male model, and Darcy decided the ladies' man label was probably more than idle banter. Her snap impression was that he was conceited and probably incapable of being faithful to one woman.

"You're even lovelier in person than on television," Leonard said smoothly, grasping Darcy's hand and holding it a little too long.

"Thank you," Darcy murmured, already turning her attention to Whiteley. Men like Dan Leonard stirred not a modicum of interest in her. "Mr. Whiteley, I'm very pleased to meet you. I understand you and Zach discussed me recently."

"Dan," Zach said, "I want to ask you about a patient..." He had gripped Dan's arm firmly and was taking him aside.

"We did, Miss Gilbert," said Whiteley, depositing his empty cocktail glass on the table beside which he stood. "Zach made an energetic pitch for you to speak to our trauma center staff. You seem to have made a great impression on Dr. Shaffer."

"But something tells me you've decided to say no. Why, Mr. Whiteley?"

Admiration gleamed briefly in Whiteley's eyes. Probably, in his position, he was not accustomed to people asking for explanations for his decisions. "I'm sure Zach told you," he said.

"I still don't understand."

"My dear, I won't bore you with my troubles. Suffice it to say that all hospitals are suffering from shortages in funds and trained personnel. County General is suffering more than most because we draw more nonpaying patients than private hospitals. In short, we have quite enough hornets' nests to deal with at County without deliberately stirring up new ones.''

Darcy looked at him archly. ''You think I'm a rabble-rouser?''

He threw back his head and laughed. ''I'm sure you're too nice a young woman to go around looking for trouble, Miss Gilbert, but somehow you media people always seem to end up in the middle of it, anyway.'' He raised a cautionary hand. ''I understand it's your job, as mine is to protect the hospital from lawsuits.''

''I respect that. May I explain what my motivation in talking to your trauma center personnel would be?''

He looked at her shrewdly. ''No harm in that.''

''I simply want to educate them about domestic violence. It's a growing problem across the country as well as right here in Foleyville. If you'll give me five minutes, I think I can convince you that the education is desperately needed and that well-informed employees would be an asset to the hospital, not a potential cause of lawsuits.''

He took out a pipe and tapped sweet-smelling tobacco into its bowl, tamping it down. Thus occupied, he eyed Darcy consideringly. He drew a gold lighter from his pocket and lit the pipe, sucking on it to get it going. Finally, he said, ''I admire persistence, Miss Gilbert. Talk. You have your five minutes.''

Darcy had never packed so much data and earnestness into such a short span of time as she did in the next five minutes. Whiteley remained silent, smoking and listening, his face betraying no hint of how he felt about her impassioned plea.

When she was finished, he said, "Zach tells me you've spoken to groups on the subject before."

"Yes."

"You're very convincing."

"Convincing enough?"

"I'll have to reflect upon it for a while. Then I'll make my final decision. Now, I must find my wife. We'll be going in to dinner shortly."

Darcy extended her hand. "Thank you, Mr. Whiteley."

He gazed at her through a plume of smoke. "You're a very determined woman, Darcy. May I call you Darcy? If you're ever looking for a job in public relations, come to see me." Relaxing now that she'd done all she could to convince him, Darcy returned his smile.

Zach appeared at her side a moment after Whiteley left the alcove. "He's still thinking it over," Darcy told him. "He said I was convincing."

"That sounds promising," Zach murmured. "Whiteley's a tough cookie."

"He hasn't agreed yet, but I gave it my best shot."

"I'll let you know the minute he decides. It would be easier if I had your home phone number."

Darcy gazed at him for a moment, debating, then decided to give him the number, preferring not to take any more calls from him at the station under the watchful eyes and alert ears of Jill and Dee Dee. She borrowed Zach's pen, scribbled the number on a cocktail napkin and handed it to him. "Do we have time for another glass of wine before dinner?"

"Just," Zach said, taking her hand and blazing a path through the crowd to the bar.

When they entered the banquet hall a few minutes later, Zach scanned the room until he spotted a table with only two vacant seats remaining. "Over there," he said, gesturing. They claimed the two chairs, and Zach introduced her to the three other couples at the table, all middle-aged. Two of the women were nurses, the third a laboratory technician.

Over one of the women's shoulders, Darcy noticed Dan Leonard hesitating in the doorway. He looked toward their table with a scowl on his face. Suddenly Darcy realized why Zach had chosen this particular table. There was no chair for Dan Leonard. Amused, she smiled to herself.

Throughout the meal, their table companions peppered Darcy with questions about her job. She found it ironic that people who dealt with life and death every day of their lives obviously thought her occupation far more interesting and exciting than theirs.

There was an after-dinner speaker followed by the presentation of awards to employees for ten, fifteen, twenty and twenty-five years of service. There was little chance for private conversation with Zach until they were in his car, driving toward Darcy's apartment.

"I talked too much at dinner," Darcy lamented. "I'm sorry."

"You couldn't avoid it without being rude. They wanted to hear."

Darcy allowed herself to relax against the plush leather car seat, grateful that he understood. For a moment, her glance rested on his big, competent hands gripping the steering wheel, and a feeling of warm well-being crept over her. She shook it off.

"Have you always lived in Foleyville?" he asked suddenly.

"No, I was raised in St. Louis."

He glanced at her. "Your family's still there?"

"My parents were killed in a car crash five years ago."

"Any brothers or sisters?"

Frowning, Darcy stared at the softly lighted dash. "No. My parents were older when I was born. They'd given up expectations of having children by then, so their change-of-life baby was something of a shock."

And you felt unwanted, he thought, hearing the wistful note in her voice. "My mother had a child when she was in her forties, too. My kid sister, Linda." He was grinning. "She's a freshman at the University of Arkansas."

"You're very fond of her," Darcy observed.

A gleam of humor lit his eyes. "She's spoiled rotten, but I had my part in that. We all did, my dad, my two older sisters and I. Mom tried to be a moderating influence, but she was usually outvoted. Linda was such a loving, sunny-natured child that we couldn't deny her anything. She turned out really well, considering."

"Where do your parents live?"

"Mom's in Rogers. My father died three years ago. I still miss him."

From the warmth in his voice when he talked about them, Darcy knew that Zach's family was close and loving. For a moment, she struggled with a little kernel of envy.

In the silence, Zach felt her withdrawal. He sensed that he might have chosen a more agreeable topic of conversation than families. "Dan Leonard was taken with you," he said, mainly to keep her talking.

Darcy shook her head to dispel the feeling of bleakness that always accompanied thoughts of her parents and childhood. "Was he?" she asked indifferently.

"You didn't notice?"

She shrugged. "My mind was on making my case with Mr. Whiteley."

"I've seen that gleam in Dan's eye plenty of times before," Zach said. "So have his ex-wives, which is why he's twice divorced." A faint worried note had crept into his tone. "I'll bet he calls you next week and asks to see you."

Darcy hesitated. The concern that had come into his voice surprised her. Did he really think she'd turn him down, then go out with the likes of Dan Leonard? He caught her studying him before she could look away. She felt a strange impulse to reassure him on that particular score. "I hope he doesn't. I don't date much. I don't have time."

His eyes held hers for another instant. "I'm certain you could make the time if you wanted to."

Darcy struggled against the unsettling feeling that this man could see inside her brain. "Dan Leonard is

not my type,'' she said evenly, deliberately miscon-
struing his remark.

Zach lifted a brow. ''Who is?''

''Perhaps I don't have a type,'' she said, peeved because her voice wasn't as strong as it should have been.
Strange, she could feel her pulse hammering at her
wrists and her throat. Zach Shaffer is my type, she
thought, stunned by the clarity and strength of the
knowledge—if I had a type.

They were less than a block from her apartment,
and unconsciously, he eased the pressure of his foot on
the accelerator, not wanting the evening to end like
this. He'd had hopes, he realized now, that the time
spent together would soften her resistance to him.
''You want to know what I think?''

''I'm not sure, but go ahead.''

''Some guy sure did a job on you, Darcy,'' he said
with quiet conviction.

She sent him a sharp look. He had no right to make
her feel this sad, bitter regret. He had no right to make
her feel anything. She forced a laugh. ''Don't imagine some dark, star-crossed love in my past.''

He pulled the car to the curb in front of her apartment building and turned toward her. He extended his
arm across the back of her seat, slipping his hand beneath her hair. ''If you're trying to tell me you've
never been in love, I don't believe you. You're a warm,
passionate woman, Darcy, as much as you try to hide
it.''

She felt the light brush of his fingers at the back of
her neck and shivered. ''What I'm trying to tell you is
that my past is private.''

His fingers stilled, but they continued to touch her neck. He searched her eyes in the shadowy dimness. "All right. Your past is not open for discussion. The present is much more interesting, anyway."

She sighed, relaxing against his hand. He was a nice man, a good man. Did it really matter if she allowed herself to linger a little longer in the warm interior of the car, enveloped in the scent of fine leather upholstery and the faint piny aroma of Zach's after-shave? His fingers massaged gently, and she turned her head against his hand, looking at him with a soft smile.

"I enjoyed the evening," she murmured.

Her smile gave him pleasure. Whatever the reason, she had decided to come out from behind her defenses, however briefly. In her smile was a glimpse of a younger, happier Darcy, before whatever it was that had put the wariness and distrust in her eyes had happened.

Her eyes widened in sudden alarm as he tightened his arm around her shoulders and pulled her across the seat and against his chest. "So did I." His deep voice was husky with feeling. "Very much."

Darcy gazed into his eyes, so close to her own. "Zach—"

He lifted both hands, pushing the hair from her face. He let his fingers dive deep into it, as he'd longed to do all evening. He leaned closer, watching her lips tremble.

He lowered his head and caught the shaky exhalation of her breath in his mouth.

His lips were firm and gentle. At first they barely touched hers. They hesitated for an endless moment, then tasted again.

In the next instant, the kiss changed. His mouth crushed hers, moving lazily, as though he had forever to savor and explore. Darcy sat paralyzed, stunned. Oddly, she felt no sudden rush of fear, no panic, no hurry to break away. Since there was no aggression in the kiss, she didn't feel threatened. It was soft, warm, wet—and unbelievably arousing.

She was aware of the taste and texture of his lips. They were firm without being hard. With incredible gentleness, he nibbled at her soft bottom lip, then his tongue moved slowly, gently between her lips, the tip tracing the smooth line of her teeth, asking for entry without demanding. Languid heat rushed through Darcy, robbing her of the will to deny him. With a sigh, her lips parted, and his tongue slipped inside.

Slowly Darcy became aware that she was leaning forward, half lying on his chest, her jacket open and her breasts crushed against hard muscle. One of his hands cupped the back of her head and the other was wrapped around her waist, pulling her close. His big hand rested on the curve of her hip. Her own arms were around his waist.

How, she wondered dimly, had they shifted and fitted their bodies to each other like this without her being aware of it? She felt boneless, incapable of moving. He groaned softly and moved his mouth on hers to taste her from a different angle, and she thought no more about easing away.

She spread her hands and slid them up his back beneath his jacket, feeling the ripple of muscle and the hardness of sinew. Tentatively, she let the tip of her tongue trace his bottom lip. Unconsciously, she pressed closer and, for the first time, she began to return his kiss. Her actions seemed involuntary, beyond her control. She tasted the inside of his mouth, angling for deeper access. Her arms wrapped themselves around his neck.

Zach was acutely aware of the moment when she began to kiss him back. He felt it like a spear of lightning through his body. He followed her lead, moving his mouth to accommodate hers, sliding his tongue along hers as it explored, hesitantly at first, then with more assurance. He molded his hands to her buttocks and lifted her sideways into his lap. Then his hands slipped beneath her jacket to caress the warm, smooth length of her bare back. Her skin felt like silk.

Slowly, he moved one hand to the side of her breast. He stroked its softness and felt the tremor of her response. The hand moved again, cupping her breast, taking its fullness into his palm. The nipple was hard and raised, and he rotated his palm slowly.

A sigh of unmistakable pleasure escaped her in a warm rush against his mouth. His hands moved on to deal with the buttons that secured the halter top of her dress at the back of her neck. Then the buttons were free of their holes. His hands, at last, had access to her naked breasts.

The pleasure of her hot skin under his touch made him groan. His fingers spread as the soft weight of one breast filled his hand. His thumb rasped slowly over the taut nipple, and Darcy moaned.

She could not think. Her mind was drowning in pleasure. She didn't even hear her own groan, didn't know she'd made a sound. All of her was concentrated on the exquisitely arousing scrape of his thumb across her nipple. A flood of heat washed through her, settling in a tight, aching knot where her legs joined her body.

Her fingers kneaded the hard musculature of his back through his shirt, the nails digging in. She moved against him and, frantically, her hands gripped his head to hold it for her hungry kiss. His hand found the juncture of her thighs and rubbed the soft mound through her dress. Gasping, Darcy pressed hard against his hand, and a little cry escaped her. The ache only grew worse.

I want him. The knowledge so shocked her that she slowly swam up through the sea of exquisite pleasure clouding her brain. Gradually she realized that the top of her dress was hanging down to her waist, and that Zach's hand touched the most intimate and sensitive part of her. It was several moments before the tremors racing through her ebbed enough for her to take control of her body.

Her mouth released his with reluctance, and her hands fell away from his head. Her body still shook, but it was more with the shock of returning to reality than with passion now. She shifted away from him. Head bowed so that her hair hid her face, she tugged clumsily at her halter and fumbled at the buttons with fingers that felt like sticks of wood.

Zach dropped his head on the car seat and drew a deep, ragged breath. He struggled with thoughts he knew he could not bring to fruition, thoughts of getting out of the car and sweeping her into his arms and carrying her into her bedroom, of undressing her, of coming to know every inch of her body intimately. Thoughts of making wild, passionate love to her over and over through the long hours of the night.

Turning his head, he saw her bent forward, trying to button her dress. He closed his eyes for a moment and drew in several unsteady breaths. When he had better control of himself, he reached out and placed his hands over hers, stilling her restless fingers.

"I'll do it," he said huskily.

She lifted her head and met his gaze. She looked as dazed as he felt. He buttoned the dress and pulled her jacket collar close around her neck. Bending over, he rubbed his cheek in her hair.

"I have to go in," she whispered, her voice trembling.

He planted a gentle kiss on the top of her head and straightened. "I'll walk you to the door."

She shook her hair as though she was trying to shake his kiss out of the dark, shining waves. Or perhaps shake off what had happened. "I'd rather you didn't. If you'll just sit here until I get inside, please..."

"All right. Darcy, I'm sorry—" Sorry for what? he wondered in confusion. Not for kissing her and touching her. He'd do it all again and more, if she'd let him. No, he wasn't sorry for that, but he was sorry that she regretted it, that she wished it hadn't happened.

"We lost our heads for a few minutes. Just don't talk about it, Zach, please." She reached for the door handle. She moved sluggishly, as though weights had been attached to her limbs. She opened the door and stepped out, reaching in for her small black evening clutch. Then she slammed the door and circled in front through the beam of the headlights.

The chill of the night air shocked her out of her half daze. She ran up the steps and opened the foyer door. She stepped inside, and the door swung closed behind her. She murmured something to the bored security guard behind the desk as she passed.

She ran down the hall to her apartment, unlocked the door and stepped inside, seeking the safety of this place that was hers alone. She had never shared it with anyone. She walked through the rooms, turning on lights, and waited for its peace to enfold her.

The peace didn't come. The taste of Zach's kisses remained on her swollen lips. The heat of his hands still warmed her skin. Zach had shown her that she was still a woman. Her sexuality was not dead, as she'd thought, but merely buried under layers of compensation and denial.

Weary beyond imagining, she drifted toward her bedroom, undressing as she went, leaving her clothes where they fell and the lights on behind her. Somehow she knew the darkness wouldn't be comforting tonight. Naked, she crawled into bed, not even bothering to remove her makeup.

When was the last time she'd failed to hang her clothes on their padded hangers or the last time she'd gone to bed without going through the regimen of lotions and creams to remove her makeup and moisten her skin for the night? She couldn't remember. It had been too long. But what did it matter?

What did anything matter, she wondered desperately, except that she felt as though her world was coming apart.

Don't think about it now, she ordered herself.

Tomorrow...

She would put it all back together tomorrow.

Chapter 6

Monday was cold and dreary. In the west, an anemic sun was gradually growing dimmer beneath a front of heavy, dark clouds. Darcy watched the clouds from her apartment windows all morning, regretting that the brief Indian summer seemed to have ended.

Sunday had dragged on interminably, and she was grateful for the start of another work week, no matter what the weather. A single bright spot had illuminated her weekend. When she'd telephoned Hope House, she'd learned that Claire Champlin was still in residence and taking part in group counseling sessions.

Thunder rumbled faintly as Darcy drove away from the apartment Monday afternoon. The day mirrored her mood: the finale to her evening with Zach had left her with a vague sense of foreboding. Zach hadn't phoned Sunday, but she knew it was only a matter of time until she would have to deal with him. After Saturday night, it was going to be more difficult than ever.

Since she'd met him at the trauma center, she had felt herself being pulled to him. From the beginning, he had felt it, too, she knew. Every time she'd seen him after that, there had been a palpable tension between them that she had tried hard to deny. Saturday night that tension had burst free, revealing itself for what it was—biological craving, lust. The craving had cried out for relief, and for several mad minutes it had seemed that a few kisses would ease the tension.

But kisses hadn't been enough. They had only intensified the craving, Darcy thought gloomily, as she braked at a red light. Sunk in thought, she didn't notice the light had turned green until the driver behind her honked impatiently. She sped across the intersection and changed lanes in anticipation of her turnoff.

She hadn't experienced such raw sexual need since she'd fallen in love with Bill—no, not Bill, but her naive illusion of him. Stupidly, she had thought the need killed, or at least forever crippled, by disillusion. Zach had shown her how wrong she could be. It was still there, imprisoned inside her, looking for the crack in her resolve that would let it go free. Saturday night the crack had opened. Now that she knew it could happen, Darcy wondered desperately what was to keep it from opening again.

Distracted, she drove past the television station before she realized it and had to circle the block and return to the employee parking lot entrance, which she entered by using a coded card.

Switching off the engine, she sat for a moment in her car. Her mind still followed the path it had been exploring during the drive. She had loved Bill in the beginning as much as any misguided eighteen-year-old could. Her desire for him remained strong until his true nature began to come out, but the sex act itself had always left her feeling vaguely disappointed. Bill usually fell asleep immediately afterward, but she had lain awake wondering what all the hullabaloo was about. Finally, she decided that she had expected too much.

Until now she had not wavered in her conviction. No man before had stirred more than a pale shadow of the desire she had felt at eighteen. If ever someone did, she had told herself, she wouldn't entertain false expectations, because she knew she'd be left feeling let down. The few encounters she'd had with men while she'd been employed at the TV station—more out of curiosity than raging desire—had confirmed what she already believed: living without sex would be no great deprivation.

Then Zach came and with a few kisses made her doubt her conclusion that sex was overrated, made her wonder if perhaps it could be more than she'd ever imagined.

Shaking off the thought, Darcy got out of the car. Thank goodness for work, she thought. There was rarely time for idle speculation while she was working.

When Dan Leonard phoned later that afternoon, as Zach had predicted, Darcy made it plain that she had no interest in going out with him. Maybe she'd been more curt than was necessary, she reflected as she hung up, but she resented being reminded of Saturday night, when she'd met him.

It rained Tuesday and Wednesday, which did nothing to brighten Darcy's mood. Jill accused her of going around like a cartoon character with a cloud of gloom over her head, but she let it go at that until Thursday afternoon.

"I guess your evening with Dr. Shaffer didn't turn out so well," Jill speculated. Obviously she had decided that Darcy would never drop a hint about what was bothering her unless she probed a little.

"That may be the understatement of the decade."

"What happened?"

"Let's just say it wasn't what I expected."

"I'm sorry," Jill said, sounding as though she meant it.

Darcy shrugged, turning away. "No big deal. Not even a small one."

Jill looked as though she didn't believe it and might have said so, but Darcy was already on the telephone, double-checking data for a story.

The temperature had dropped into the thirties by the time Darcy left the station that night for her weekly stint on the hot line. In spite of the cold, she was glad she didn't have to go home just yet. Lately her evenings at home had been long and boring because she couldn't seem to settle down to doing anything. Cleaning suddenly seemed futile, since it would have to be done again in a few days. The television sitcoms she occasionally enjoyed struck her as more than ordinarily juvenile. Even listening to tales of domestic tragedy seemed preferable, and at least she'd be doing something more useful than wandering restlessly around her apartment.

Betina Meyer and Phil, the sociology student, were already on the phones when Darcy entered. Another volunteer was pouring three cups of coffee from a fresh pot. "Want a cup?" she asked as Darcy hung her coat on a hook.

"Yes, thanks," Darcy said, rubbing her hands together. "Brr, it's getting cold." She accepted the warm mug from the woman gratefully and carried it to her usual spot.

"Always does this time of year," the woman said without cracking a smile. Darcy raised an eyebrow and glanced at Betina, who sat at the other end of Darcy's table.

"How's it going tonight?" Darcy asked as Betina hung up her phone and lit a cigarette.

"Not too bad. We don't have calls backed up for a change." Betina lounged in her chair and drew on her cigarette. "Do you think warm weather is more conducive to violence that cold?"

"Sounds reasonable," Darcy agreed. She took a sip of her coffee, and the telephone rang. She set down her cup. "I'll get this one," she said, lifting the receiver. "Domestic violence hot line."

"I want to speak to—uh, just a minute—to Jo."

They seemed to have a bad connection. The caller was difficult to understand, but Darcy was sure it was a man. More men called the hot line than one might think, some because they wanted to stop battering, others to ask advice on what to do about a battering situation they suspected in their family or among friends.

Darcy had even talked to one man whose wife attacked him with whatever was handy when she was angry. She'd given him numerous cuts and bruises, and once a broken nose. He'd said he didn't want to leave her, and he hadn't asked for advice on how to make her stop attacking him. He'd simply wanted help in learning to recognize when an outburst was imminent so he could get out of her way.

"Speaking," Darcy said.

"Jo?"

Darcy raised her voice a notch. "Yes, this is Jo."

"You think you're hot stuff, don't you?"

"What?" She wasn't sure she'd heard him correctly. His voice sounded muffled, far away.

"Think you can tell people what to do—"

"I don't know what you're talking about."

"My life! You can't ruin my life and get away with it! Nobody treats me like scum and gets away with it. You better believe it!"

Darcy felt a shiver of alarm. "I'm sorry, I think you have the wrong Jo."

"I got the right one, all right. Listen, you're gonna pay. Count on it. I'll—"

Darcy hung up. She stared at her hand on the receiver, then pulled it away. Goose bumps had broken out on her arms beneath her long-sleeved sweater.

At the other end of the table, Betina said goodbye to her caller and replaced the receiver. "You okay, Darcy?"

"Sure. It was just some nut." She'd talked to mentally disturbed people before, most of the volunteers had. Why was she letting this one get to her?

"What'd he say?"

"He accused me of ruining his life."

"Classic paranoid delusion," Betina said. "Probably thought he was talking to God—or his mother."

But he had asked for Jo. "Probably," Darcy murmured.

Betina took a call then, and Darcy took one a moment later. They had few idle minutes for the rest of the shift; but at three o'clock, when she walked out to the parking lot with Betina and Phil, Darcy still hadn't shaken the uneasy feeling left by that phone call.

Driving home, she finally admitted to herself why she was uneasy. She couldn't rid herself of the suspicion that the threatening caller was Bill. His accusations had sounded all too familiar. Before she left Bill, he had repeatedly accused her of thinking she was too good for him, of ill using him, even of destroying his life. And she'd been involved with no one else deeply enough for any other man to imagine she'd had such a drastic effect on his life.

She hadn't recognized the voice, but she no longer thought they'd had a bad connection. She believed the caller had deliberately disguised his voice, probably by placing a cloth over the receiver, lowering the tone and changing the inflection. Would he have bothered if he hadn't thought she'd recognize his normal voice?

She had no idea how Bill could have discovered that she worked on the hot line Thursday nights or that she was known to callers as Jo; but she had no trouble believing he could do it. When she left him, she found out how relentless he could be in pursuit of a goal. He'd tracked her down wherever she happened to be. She'd even moved twice to get away from him, and each time he'd found her.

As a last resort, she'd filed a complaint and got a restraining order. He'd ignored that, too, until she finally called the police and they took him away. In all, she'd endured more than six months of harassment before he left town—on advice of the police, she'd always thought.

When she graduated and went to work for the TV station, she'd moved to her present apartment. By then, the passage of time had convinced her he'd given up any hope that they could get back together. Still, she'd chosen a building with a security guard on duty around the clock, just in case Bill ever decided to come back.

Now he *was* back. When he showed up at the sidewalk café last week, she'd assured herself he couldn't know where she lived now, but that had been whistling in the dark. If he could find out where she was on Thursday nights and that she used the pseudonym Jo, he could find out where she lived.

Driving across town on near-deserted streets, she searched her rearview mirror repeatedly for headlights. But she wasn't followed. Still, she was enormously relieved when she was inside her apartment with the doors locked and bolted. Anyone entering the building through the foyer had to pass the security guard at the desk. Nonresidents were asked to identify themselves and the person they'd come to see, then wait while the guard cleared the visit with the resident.

The courtyard in back was surrounded by a ten-foot-high solid wood fence, its gates padlocked. The guard on duty patrolled the perimeter of the fence and building every hour, leaving the foyer entrance door locked until he returned. Not that it was impossible to scale the fence when the guard wasn't looking...

You have to stop this, she told herself. If she didn't, she would be reduced to a quivering knot of nerves by daybreak. She made sure all the windows were locked and the blinds and draperies closed before undressing.

As she was tying the belt of her wraparound satin robe, the telephone rang. The sound was shrill and jarring in the silent apartment, one of twelve apartments in the hushed building where, she was sure, everyone else but the security guard was asleep.

Bill! she thought instantly. Dear God, did he know her unlisted phone number, too? She stared at the instrument beside her bed for a few moments, as though she expected it to sprout legs and come after her. It kept ringing. If she didn't answer, he'd keep calling back. She knew him.

She snatched up the receiver. "Hello," she said, her voice cracking with strain.

"Darcy?"

"Zach!" Relief washed through her, and she slumped down on the bed.

"I didn't wake you, did I?"

"No."

"I remember you saying you work on the hot line until three Friday mornings. I took a chance I could catch you before you went to bed."

She waited, letting the normality of his voice, of Zach himself, enfold her. If it had been Bill . . .

"Darcy, did you hear me?"

"Uh, sorry. What was it again?"

"Do you have a copy of your lecture on domestic violence?"

She struggled to focus her mind on what he was saying. After the anxiety of the last few hours, the ordinariness of it was like a breath of fresh air in a stifling room. "Yes, I do."

"Whiteley wants to see it. I think he's leaning in our direction, but he wants to be assured there's nothing in your remarks that might be construed as irresponsible. That's his word, not mine."

"If he finds something irresponsible, he'll ask me to take it out, right? That's censorship."

"I know it is, but I don't see any way around it if you want to talk to the employees."

"Well, it seems to be the lesser of two evils. I'll mail him a copy tomorrow."

"He'd like to see it tomorrow morning."

"Oh, Zach," Darcy said, sighing, "I won't be awake until noon." If she managed to sleep at all. "I suppose I could take it out to the hospital before I go to the station, if I can work it in. I can't promise, though."

"I have an idea. My shift just ended and I'm going somewhere for a bite to eat. If you aren't too tired— well, I thought you might be hungry, too. You could meet me and bring the speech. There's an all-night diner two blocks north of your apartment. Maxie's. Know it?''

"I've seen it."

"Will you come?"

A reprieve, Darcy thought. Before tonight she would have been hesitant to expose herself so soon again to the danger Zach represented. But it was a different kind of danger from the one that had hovered over her since the threatening phone call, a danger that she conceivably had some control over. The other was irrational, unpredictable and terrifying because it had no definite shape. Almost anything was preferable to staying in the apartment with that fear.

"How soon can you be there?" she asked finally.

"Twenty minutes." She heard the leap of elation in his voice. He hadn't thought she'd say yes.

"See you then, Zach." She hung up and threw off her robe. She dressed in jeans and a bulky yellow sweater, not bothering with a bra. Still fifteen minutes to go, and she could get there in less than five. She decided she'd rather wait at the diner. Grabbing a navy wool pea jacket and her purse, she went out into the cold night.

She felt exposed, driving to the diner. For a few moments, she even imagined that a dark sedan was following her. But the car turned off before she reached her destination. She climbed out and hurried toward the lighted diner, the collar of her jacket pulled up against the wind. She had to get herself in hand, she reflected, as she reached the door.

She forced herself to think about her fear rationally. She didn't know for sure it was Bill who'd made the call. It could have been a nut with a grudge against the world, as Betina had said. In that case, he might know her pseudonym without knowing her true identity.

There was no one in the diner except a bored-looking man reading a true crime magazine behind the lunch counter. He nodded and asked what he could get her. She said she was meeting someone and would wait. It was warm in the diner, and she shrugged out of her jacket, aware of the counterman watching her curiously from behind his magazine.

Zach drove a bit faster than the law allowed to reach the diner, fearing she wouldn't be there, after all. If she was, he didn't want to keep her waiting, give her time to reflect and reverse her decision to meet him.

There had been something odd in her voice on the telephone. She was probably still disturbed by what had happened between them Saturday night, and embarrassed by her response. He'd decided the odds of her agreeing to meet him tonight were probably ninety-five percent against. Her yes had rekindled the flame of optimism that her Saturday-night leave-taking had doused.

He let out a deep breath when he entered the diner and saw her sitting at a table, chin resting in her hands.

"Hi." He sat down.

She looked up and he felt a subtle increase in her alertness. She smiled tiredly.

"Hi." He looked boyish in faded jeans and a leather jacket open over a red-plaid flannel shirt.

He took off his jacket. "Have you ordered?"

Her shoulders lifted a little. "I waited for you." She slid several folded sheets of paper across the table.

He stuffed the copy of her speech in the pocket of his jacket. "The chili's good here."

"That sounds great. I'd like milk to drink. I didn't realize how hungry I was until I got here."

Zach asked the counterman for two bowls of chili and two glasses of milk. Returning his gaze to Darcy, he said, "I've wanted to call you ever since Saturday night, but I wasn't sure you wanted to hear from me. Asking you to meet me here—it was a shot in the dark. I didn't think you'd come."

She thought the less said about Saturday night, the better. "I didn't want to stay in the apartment," she said candidly. "I knew I wouldn't be able to sleep, anyway. It's been one of those nights."

It wasn't really an explanation, but he detected an anxious note in her tone. He also noticed a faint tremor in her fingers as she reached for a paper napkin from the dispenser. Something was bothering her that had nothing to do with him. He reached across the table and enveloped both her hands in his. They were cold.

"What happened tonight?" he asked gently.

She searched the clear blue depths of his eyes, and he smiled encouragingly. She was all too aware that, regardless of their short acquaintance, he was more sensitive to her moods than her closest friend. She had thought earlier that his attraction made him danger-ous, but in spite of that she knew instinctively that she could trust him. She sensed a strength that had nothing to do with his size; it exercised a calming effect on her.

She relaxed, feeling the warmth and protection of his hands enclosing hers. "I received a crank call on the hot line tonight. Ever since, I've been imagining villains in dark corners."

He slowly rubbed his thumbs over the backs of her hands, soothing away the little knots of tension. "What did he say? I assume it was a man."

"Yes," she admitted with a sigh. "He said I'd ruined his life and that he'd make me pay."

He frowned and his thumbs stilled. "Was it someone you know?"

Her soft mouth tightened and she hesitated a beat before answering. "I can't be sure. He didn't give his name, of course."

Her hands clenched involuntarily in his. His fingers resumed their slow massage. "But he knew yours?"

"We use pseudonyms on the hot line. He asked for Jo. That's me." She forced her hands to relax in his. "I'm letting it bother me more than it should. We get calls from men occasionally, so I might have talked to him before. That could be why he asked for Jo."

He knew from the bleak look in her eyes that she was still worried nevertheless. "Did he indicate how he would make you pay, or when?"

She shook her head. "I hung up."

The counterman was heading for the table with their order. Zach released her hands reluctantly and drew back to make room for the steaming bowls of chili and tall glasses of milk. When the man retreated, Zach said, "Maybe you should talk to the police about it."

The chili smelled wonderful. She dipped her spoon into it. "What could they do?"

"Maybe they'd put a tap on the line."

She reflected for a moment. "Then we'd have to inform all hot line callers that the line was tapped. Most of them would probably hang up right then." She frowned. "But if he calls again, I may talk to the police just to get it on record." She took a bite and found the chili tasted every bit as good as it smelled. "Mmm, I needed this. I feel better already."

She wanted to put the phone call out of her mind, he realized, and set about helping her. "A man brought his wife to the trauma center tonight. She'd swallowed a full bottle of aspirin tablets."

"He must have been terrified."

"No, he was fighting mad. While we pumped her stomach, he hung over her yelling into her ear." Zach pushed his voice several notes higher, imitating the man. " 'There! How does that feel? Does that feel good? I guess you'll take another bottle of aspirin real soon, won't you? Be sure and get one of those name brands. They cost more! While you're at it, get a bottle for your mother, too!' "

Darcy couldn't suppress a giggle at the picture his words painted. "Not exactly sympathetic, was he?"

The tension easing out of her face told him he'd been successful in diverting her thoughts, temporarily. "It turned out she'd made certain she wouldn't be in any real danger. She swallowed the tablets in front of him after he called her mother a nagging old witch.''

Darcy shook her head wonderingly. "I guess you see all kinds in the emergency room.''

"Yeah," he said, and went on to relate a few of the other amusing incidents that occasionally relieved the life-and-death intensity under which he worked.

When they were ready to leave, Darcy said, "You've taken my mind off my troubles. Thank you, Zach.''

"I'll follow you home," he said firmly, "so you won't have to worry about villains.''

It was a measure of her underlying concern that she didn't argue with him. When they reached the apartment building, he parked his car beside hers and got out to walk her to her door. He expected a quick goodnight at the door, but when they got there, she said a bit shamefacedly, "Would you mind waiting just a minute, until I look around?''

"I'll do better than that. I'll check it out for you.''

They went inside and took off their jackets. She followed him as he looked in all the rooms, including the closets. "All clear," he said.

He turned from inspecting the last closet to find her standing close behind him. "You're sweet to humor me. I feel pretty foolish. We have good security here.''

He'd been glad to see that guard in the lobby; the guard made him feel better about leaving her alone. But he also knew that some of the worst fears weren't overcome by reasonable safeguards like security guards.

It seemed the most natural thing in the world to wrap his arms around her. "It's not foolish to need reassurance once in a while." She looked up at him almost desolately. He saw desire mixed with a desperate uncertainty in her wide eyes. With a sigh of understanding, he folded her against him.

"You were a godsend tonight," she murmured. She laid her cheek on his broad chest with a faint sound that might have been a whimper or a moan.

Zach lifted his hand to thread his fingers through her hair. "We aim to please, ma'am," he said, the lightness of the words belied by their husky rasp. He combed through silky strands, pausing to trace the curve of her ear with his thumb. He placed a lingering kiss on top of her head.

His warm breath on her hair made Darcy shiver. "You make me feel safe even while you scare me to death," she whispered. "It's very confusing."

His gentle laughter was a warm caress in her hair. "I *scare* you? You continually surprise me, Darcy. I'm a harmless guy."

She smiled and lifted her hands to place them on his chest. "About as harmless as a hawk in a chicken house." She struggled against a feeling of desolation as she pushed away from him and turned.

He stopped her walking away by wrapping his arm around her breasts and closing his other hand over her shoulder. He waited to see what she would do. She stood still, her head bowed, and he exerted pressure to draw her against him. She relaxed against his chest. "I make you feel things you don't want to feel," he said quietly. "What I don't understand is why you don't want to."

Darcy brought her hand up and caressed the fingers spread over her rib cage at the side of her breast. Briefly, she pressed her cheek against the hand that still clasped her shoulder. "I know you don't," she said, sighing. "I wish—"

His arm brushed her breasts as he lifted his hand to guide her head to the hollow of his shoulder. Then his palm covered her heart, and he felt its fast beat. "What do you wish?"

She laughed softly, helplessly. "That I'd met you eleven years ago, I guess."

He dropped his hands to slip them beneath her sweater. She wore no bra, and he touched her breasts gently. "Eleven? That's an odd number to pull out of the air."

She closed her eyes as the languid weakness of sexual desire stole over her. The sensations produced by his hands moving on her breasts were so intense they robbed her of speech.

He knew she hadn't pulled the number out of the air; it had slipped out before she had realized it. The thing that stood between them, the thing she guarded so zealously, had happened eleven years ago.

Later he would try to figure it out. Right now he couldn't figure out the way to the bathroom. The ache in his groin took all his attention. He spread his legs and pulled her into the saddle thus formed, trying to assuage the ache. It made it worse.

She battled the need to grind her hips against his hardness. There would be no turning back then. She'd let it go too far as it was.

"Zach..." She stopped to swallow the breathless catch in her voice.

Her mixed emotions were communicated to him without her saying any more. He relaxed the arm that held her hard against him. But he couldn't stop touching her completely, not yet.

He lifted the hair from her neck, bent and investigated her nape with his tongue. "I make a good bodyguard. I could spend the night and watch over you. Not that I think you really need one with the security you have here, but if it'll make you feel better..." His whispered voice trembled across her flesh. The clean scent of her skin dizzied him.

"I don't...think that's...a good idea." Her inability to think and speak coherently frightened her.

His mouth, which had been nibbling her neck, stilled. "I guess not." She was particularly vulnerable tonight, and he might be able to change her mind. But it wouldn't be fair. There could be no deceit, no manipulation between them. She was too good for anything less that perfect honesty.

He wanted her—oh, God, how he wanted her—but she had to want him too, without any reservations. She still had those in abundance.

Later, when the time was right, he would drive out every reservation and show her the pure and fiery rapture of two people giving themselves, body and soul, equally. At the moment, he had no trouble believing that time would come. Doubt would arise later, when he was alone.

He lifted his head and ran his hands up and down her arms soothingly. After a few minutes, he felt the feverish heat in her body ebb, and she grew calm. He took a deep breath and stepped back.

She turned and looked up at him, her dark eyes remorseful. "Thank you," she said simply.

He brushed his knuckles under her chin, clamping down on his need. "You can always call me if you change your mind about the bodyguard."

Chapter 7

Because twenty-four to thirty-six-hour shifts had been the rule during his residency days, Zach had long ago acquired the skill of closing his eyes, blanking his mind and falling instantly asleep. But tonight the skill deserted him. He rolled out of bed, pulled on sweats and running shoes and went to the kitchen to make hot chocolate.

He carried his cup to the glassed-in portion of the patio attached to the back of his town house. He flopped in a leather lounge chair with a raised foot-rest. He tried to tell himself that the persistent ache in his groin was merely the result of his not having a woman for several months.

The last time had been with the divorcée he'd been seeing for almost a year, and even then he'd known that relationship was over. In the beginning, he'd thought she wanted no more than he did—occasional companionship and physical intimacy without any deep emotional attachment. When he realized she was hoping for more, he'd seen her one last time, wanting to let her down as gently as he could. But she'd seemed not to understand what he'd been driving at all evening, and he'd decided he ought in fairness to give her a little more time to grow accustomed to the idea.

The next morning, she'd wakened him with a farm-hand's breakfast on a tray and a confidence in her smile that hadn't been there the night before. He'd known then that he would only be hurting her more by prolonging the charade. A clean break would be kinder in the end. He'd told her flatly that it was over and had left without breakfast. She'd cried, and he'd felt like a total heel.

It had been the longest ongoing relationship he'd had with a woman. As far as he was concerned, the longevity resulted from convenience rather than emotional commitment, but apparently the reverse had been true for her. The feeling that he might have unintentionally led her to believe he was more involved than was the case kept him from even looking for someone else. Once burned, twice shy, as his mother used to say.

He hadn't been looking for Darcy, either. She'd simply appeared as if conjured by some perverse fairy godmother, and he'd known the first night that she could be much more than a convenience to him. Until tonight, he hadn't been sure the strong sexual attraction he felt was reciprocated.

The long, loose sweater she'd worn—by design, he suspected—had camouflaged the ripe curves beneath, but he'd had no trouble imagining them. To his surprise, she hadn't protested when his hands slipped beneath the camouflage to fit around her bare breasts.

His fingers curled tightly around his mug, as if they were again accepting the feminine weight. The porcelain was warm and hard against his palm, as the taut nipple had been, but smooth instead of dimpled. Her skin was incredibly soft, and when he touched her he never wanted to stop. Even her scent aroused him.

No other woman could satisfy him now. It was Darcy he craved. He sipped his chocolate, imagining her naked, beneath him. His hands would learn the exact contour of her legs, her tight buttocks. How would the satiny skin stretched over her flat stomach taste? And the soft flesh on the inside of her thighs?

He imagined her moaning as he took his time finding out, her skin heating in pleasured reaction. He imagined her reaching for him, locking her legs around him. He imagined her moving with him, her sweet cries in his ear begging him to release her in one breath, and in the next to hold her forever in the wild pleasure that was driving them both out of their minds. His groin throbbed in futile response.

She had wanted him tonight. He could have taken her. But it would have been only her body he had, and he would never be satisfied with that. Moreover, his own satisfaction wasn't of first importance. Beneath her self-reliance, her guardedness with him—with all men, he suspected—he sensed something exquisitely fragile, perhaps broken and not yet fully healed.

She had not revealed a single intimate detail of her personal life. She had agreed to the few meetings they'd had only because she wanted to speak to the trauma center employees. She'd given him her unlisted phone number for the same reason. He suspected she would not have agreed to see him tonight if she hadn't been upset over the crank phone call. She'd been less guarded tonight for the same reason.

Before he took her body, he wanted her trust. She had been hurt, and he wanted to protect her from further pain. He wanted her to find safety in his arms.

At the age of thirty-four, he had found a woman whose needs superceded his own. He wasn't sure what that meant in terms of his own needs and feelings. He wasn't entirely comfortable even exploring the question. He knew that sex with Darcy would touch him in places that had never been touched, involve emotions that had lain dormant, waiting, until now. He could teach her what it meant to go beyond sex to lovemaking. But it would be a violation if he pressed her to that point too soon, before she was sure she could trust him with her essential innocence and vulnerability.

Zach sat in the darkness, drinking his chocolate, letting his mind absorb what his instincts already knew. The right moment would come, and he would recognize it. Knowing it would be worth the wait eased some of the ache in his gut. When he returned to his bed, he was able to sleep.

Darcy finished her third cup of coffee since coming to work and grimaced as she set the empty cup on her desk. There was a burning in her stomach, and she felt a bit queasy. Too much coffee, she told herself. The past week, her appetite had flagged, and she'd skipped meals, substituting innumerable cups of coffee. She wasn't sure whether it was the threatening phone call last Thursday night or her increasingly confused feelings about Zach that had robbed her of hunger and stretched her nerves to the breaking point. Probably both, she thought gloomily.

She hadn't heard from Zach in a week, and she was beginning to suspect the hospital administrator had decided against letting her speak to the hospital employees. She would have thought Zach would give her the disappointing news as soon as he heard it, though. Maybe the administrator was still undecided, even after reading her speech.

For a moment, she toyed with the idea of phoning Zach to find out what was going on. Then she decided against it, partially because she wasn't sure how hearing Zach's voice would affect her. She wasn't sure of much these days. Before she met Zach, she'd never had any trouble knowing her own mind.

She pulled her thoughts away from Zach and centered them on her visit yesterday with Claire Champlin at Hope House. After a week, Claire had moved her children into the shelter with her. Yesterday she'd told Darcy that she had no immediate plans to leave. She found the presence of other women like herself unexpectedly comforting, and she was gaining new insights into her marriage and her own psyche through her counseling sessions. She hadn't heard from Ralph, she told Darcy, which meant he still didn't know where she and the children were. Darcy only hoped he wouldn't find out before Claire's tentative explora-

tions into herself had been transformed into a revital-
ized self-image and positive plans for the future.

"Darcy, read this and see if there's anything else you
want to add to the story."

Jill's voice jolted Darcy from her ruminations.
"You startled me," she murmured. "I didn't see you
coming." She took the sheet of paper from Jill's hand
and scanned it. She was almost through when the
telephone rang and, once more, her heart leaped and
she started.

"Boy, are you jumpy," Jill said. "What's—"

A woman's raised voice interrupted. "Darcy, it's for
you. Zach Shaffer."

Jill's eyes widened in curiosity. "I thought that was
off."

Darcy reached for the phone. "It was never on—not
the way you mean." She wondered if Jill could detect
any hint of the mixed emotions accompanying that
statement. "Excuse me, Jill." She picked up the receiver. "Hello, Zach." Jill walked away slowly and
with obvious reluctance.

"Hi, Darcy. How are you?"

"Well. And you?"

"Walking in my sleep. I've worked a couple of
double shifts this week. There's a twenty-four-hour
virus going through the medical staff."

"You'd better take care of yourself." As soon as she
said it, she was sure she sounded presumptuous.

Zach didn't seem to notice. "I have next weekend
off. If I didn't have that to look forward to, I'd col-
lapse in my tracks right now."

Darcy forced back an impulse to ask if he was eating properly.

"I just talked to Whiteley. He says you can speak to the trauma center staff."

"Oh, that's good news, Zach. I'd almost given up."

"So had I. I've been looking at the schedules, and it appears Saturday afternoon is the best time. If that doesn't interfere with your plans."

"Saturday will be fine. What time?"

"How about four o'clock in the hospital's education center? I'll meet you in the south lobby."

"Okay. I—I'm looking forward to it, Zach." She heard an ambulance siren in the background.

"So am I. Ah," he said sighing, "they're playing my song again. I have to go. See you Saturday, Darcy."

He hung up before she had time to say goodbye. Pensively, she replaced the receiver. Zach's phone call had eased the vague sense of apprehension that had made her feel on edge the past week. She was finally able to admit that she'd been worried she'd alienated him Thursday night by asking him to leave. But he hadn't sounded alienated, only tired.

Darcy didn't understand herself. She couldn't bring herself to contemplate intimacy with Zach, and the emotional upheaval she knew somehow it would entail. Yet the thought of never seeing him again or hearing his voice made her feel bereft.

Strangely, her appetite returned that afternoon, and she ate a hearty, if hasty, dinner with Jill at a nearby restaurant between the six and ten o'clock programs. She didn't even mind Jill's questions about Zach, not much, anyway. But she hastened to correct Jill's assumption that a romance was developing.

"It's business, I keep telling you," Darcy said. "I'm talking about domestic violence to the trauma center personnel Saturday. Zach called to set the time and place."

"You ought to see yourself when you talk about him. You get that little, secret smile and your eyes go all dreamy."

"That's the silliest thing I ever heard," Darcy sputtered.

"Then why are you blushing?"

"I'm not—I—oh, shut up."

Jill stopped teasing her, to Darcy's enormous relief. At the station there was no time for personal conversation, and after the ten o'clock report, Darcy left immediately for her Thursday-night shift on the hot line.

The call was Darcy's fourth of the night.

"Jo, you know who this is."

Her heart skipped a beat, then seemed to hurl itself against her eardrums. The man's voice was muffled and indistinct, but she recognized it as the same voice that had threatened her a week ago.

She forced herself to speak slowly and calmly. "Who is this?"

He laughed, an evil sound.

"What do you want?"

"I'll let you know what I want—soon. I just wanted to tell you I haven't forgotten you. I think about you all the time, Jo. I think about what I'll do to you.

You'll pay for ruining my life—'' The words came faster, tumbling over each other, pushed by hate.

A cold chill shuddered through Darcy. "I reported you to the police," she said. "If you don't want to be caught, don't call here again." She hung up and covered her face with her hands.

Beside her, Betina asked, "Was that the same nut who called last week?"

Darcy nodded, shivering. She lifted her head.

"Hey, he really got to you. Maybe you *should* report it to the police."

"What can they do? I can't tell them who he is." Betina was right. The caller was getting under her skin, and she was angry with herself for letting him. It was Bill, she was sure of it. He'd destroyed her life once. Was she going to let him do it again?

What she had to do, she told herself, was convince him—and herself—that she wasn't the same helplessly passive woman she'd been when they were married. She thought of the small Mace canister Jill carried in her purse for protection, and decided she'd buy one for herself the next day. Having finally made a decision to defend herself aggressively, if she had to, she felt more in control of the situation.

"I'm all right," she told Betina, who was still watching her with concern. "If I can't cope with calls from crazies, I have no business being on the hot line."

"This has been needed for so long," a young nurse told Darcy. "I grew up in a home where my father battered my mother, and I know that helpless feeling you talked about." She looked around at her companions and a flush crept up her neck. "That's the first time I ever said that aloud."

Darcy squeezed the young nurse's hand as though to say, I understand. And she did. Sometimes it took hearing someone talk about other battering situations to give a person the courage to admit to having lived in such a home.

Darcy's talk to the trauma center personnel had gone well. They had listened attentively, and afterward, kept her there with questions for another half hour. A few people, including the young nurse, had gathered around Darcy with more questions after the others had left.

"I'd like to talk to someone about volunteering on the Domestic Violence Hot Line," an older woman said.

Darcy wrote the director's name and phone number on the back of a business card and gave it to her. "We always need more help. Thanks for considering it."

Zach stood to one side until everyone else had left. Then he got Darcy's coat and helped her into it. "You were great. You could've heard a pin drop while you were talking." He lifted her hair, letting it fall outside the coat collar. His hands lingered on her shoulders for a moment before they dropped away.

"They did seem very interested," Darcy agreed, turning to smile at him. He looked relaxed in khaki-colored cords and a gold crewneck sweater. "Did you catch up on your sleep?"

He gave her a wry smile. "Twelve hours last night. I was dead. Fortunately, everybody's on his feet again so I shouldn't have to work any more double shifts for a while."

"Good. I—" She halted, faintly flustered. She'd almost said she'd been worried about him. "You're lucky you didn't catch the virus."

He wondered idly what she'd stopped herself from saying. "The business office will mail your stipend after the first of the month, but I want to give you a token of my appreciation now."

"Oh?" She looked up at him, touched but a bit wary. "What did you have in mind?"

One corner of his mouth quirked in a smile. "Dinner at my place."

It sounded wonderful. Darcy was amazed at *how* wonderful it sounded, but she couldn't accept. Being alone with Zach at his place would be like throwing herself into his arms, which also sounded wonderful, but unwise. He made her want him, and then he took away her resolve. "I can't, Zach."

"Do you have other plans?"

"No—"

"If you're worried about being lured into the beast's den, we won't be alone." She returned his smile. "My mother and kid sister came down for the weekend. Mom's making her famous barbecued brisket. I told her I hoped to bring somebody back with me."

Darcy relaxed. She wasn't crazy about the prospect of spending another evening alone in her apartment, jumping every time the phone rang for fear the anonymous caller had somehow tracked her down. "In that case, I suppose I can come, after all."

He grinned and extended his hand. She linked her fingers through his, and they went out of the trauma center. Darcy left her car there and rode with Zach. But on the drive, she began to have misgivings about accepting Zach's invitation. Would his mother and sister assume she and Zach were involved in a serious relationship if Zach brought her to dinner? She decided she had no control over what they assumed, and it wasn't her business to set them straight. Zach could do that if he wanted to.

Still, she felt a bit tense and uneasy about her reception as Zach ushered her into an attractive, new town house. She had a fleeting impression of lots of stained wood and glass, gray carpets and upholstery in shades of gray and blue, then Zach was introducing her to a matronly looking woman whose red hair was peppered with silver.

"Call me Maggie," she said, extending her hand. "I'm glad you could come for dinner, Darcy."

Zach threw his arm around a tall, auburn-haired young woman of about nineteen, hugging her fondly. "This is the brat, Darcy. Linda, this is Darcy Gilbert."

Linda jabbed Zach's ribs with her elbow and he grimaced. She smiled at Darcy. "Older brothers are such a pain. Hi, Darcy. It's a pleasure to meet you."

"Come on into the dining room," Maggie Shaffer said. "I just have to set the food on the table."

Linda stood on tiptoe and whispered something in Zach's ear, then giggled and ran after her mother. Darcy waited while Zach put their coats away. "I like them," she whispered as he closed the closet door. "What did Linda say to you just now?"

He smoothed her hair back, framing her face with his big hands. The corners of his eyes crinkled in amusement. "She said you were too classy for me. Revenge for calling her a brat." He let his hands drop.

Laughing, Darcy walked into the dining room ahead of him. The meal was delicious. Darcy told Zach's mother so several times, which seemed to please her. She felt none of the discomfort she had expected to feel with Zach's family. They drew her into the conversation, and she found herself talking and laughing along with the others.

There were a few tense moments, for Darcy at least, when Maggie and Linda got into a heated discussion over a speeding ticket Linda had apparently received before they left for Foleyville.

"That's why we had to take the bus here," Linda said, including both Darcy and Zach in her put-upon glance. "The bus! Can you believe it? *She* wouldn't let me drive. Don't you think that's a bit much?"

"No comment," said Zach judiciously.

"I have no opinion," Darcy added.

Linda sighed heavily. "She says I can't use the car for a week! I guess I'll have to thumb my way to school Monday."

"You can easily get a ride with one of your friends," Maggie said. "And you knew what the punishment would be if you got another speeding ticket, young lady. I told you plainly when you got the last one."

Linda put up a heated argument, but Maggie held firm. While that was going on, Zach lifted his shoulders and grinned at Darcy. She concentrated on eating, expecting any minute for Linda to storm out of the room. But that didn't happen. Linda voiced her opinion several times that the punishment was too harsh, and Maggie disagreed just as animatedly.

By the time the meal was over and Darcy was helping the other two women clear the table, Maggie and Linda were talking and laughing together like the best of friends.

As soon as the dishes were in the dishwasher, Linda asked, "Zach, can Mom and I use your car to run to the mall?"

"I'll do the driving," Maggie said.

Linda rolled her eyes. "You wouldn't drive to Foleyville, but you'll drive to the mall."

"You know I don't like driving long distances," Maggie said reasonably. "I'll drive to the mall because you aren't going to drive Zach's car when you're forbidden to drive yours." She glanced at Zach. "If Zach doesn't mind, that is. We need to find a dress for Linda's sorority's holiday banquet."

Zach pulled his keys from his trousers pocket and tossed them to his mother. "Be my guest."

Linda dashed out of the room in search of their coats. "We won't be gone long," Maggie said.

It appeared that she would be staying for a while, Darcy thought, since Zach's was the only car available. Perhaps she should have driven her own car. Not that she was worried about being alone with Zach. Maggie had said they wouldn't be gone long.

Hearing the front door close behind Maggie and Linda, Darcy curled into a corner of the couch in Zach's den. He watched her from across the room, then smiled lazily and joined her.

Her arm lay along the top of the couch. He reached up and covered her hand with his. "They're kind of overwhelming sometimes."

Darcy smiled. "I think they're wonderful."

He watched her intently. "I sensed their arguing during dinner made you uncomfortable."

"It surprised me. Your family's so different from mine. My parents allowed no arguments. It used to frustrate me terribly. Whenever I voiced a disagreement, I got the silent treatment. It's hard to disagree with someone who won't answer you." She'd vowed things would be different when she married, that disagreements would be brought into the open. But it hadn't been that way, because disagreements with Bill ultimately led to violence. "Your family's way is healthier."

An odd sadness clouded her eyes. Zach rubbed the back of his hand gently over her cheek, then curled his fingers loosely around the side of her neck. "We were always a noisy bunch. When we were all at home, it got pretty hectic at times. We talked things out—" he grinned "—sometimes yelled them out, and things got settled in the end. My parents were great talkers, but they didn't believe in corporal punishment. Neither of them ever laid a hand on me or my sisters."

She reached up and clasped the fingers that were rubbing the side of her neck. She lowered his hand to her lap, enclosing it between her hands. She didn't look at him.

"Darcy," he said quietly, "I didn't know they were planning to go out when I invited you to dinner."

She looked up, held his eyes with hers. "I wasn't thinking you planned this. I'm sure you don't have to scheme to get a woman alone. Honestly, it's all right, Zach." She felt the tension she always felt between them when they were alone. She smiled tremulously. His eyes were like blue velvet, gentle but grave, unsmiling.

He didn't have to scheme to get other women alone, but Darcy was another matter. He truly hadn't known his mother and sister would decide to go shopping, but he was enormously grateful they had.

They looked at each other for a long moment, their eyes questioning. Then, as if by common agreement, they reached for each other. She didn't know who moved first, but one hand curved over a broad shoulder, her other rested on his square jaw, her thumb sliding over the bone, feeling the slight coarseness of his skin. His hand cupped her face, his long fingers tangling in her hair. Neither of them spoke. For an instant, they were still, staring at each other. Her mouth parted slightly, and slowly he lowered his head.

There was no hesitation, no tentativeness in the moment their lips joined. His tongue plunged deeply into her mouth as if it belonged there, and her mouth welcomed it. Yet it was not a hurried kiss. They lingered over it, content for the moment to explore anew the taste of each other. Darcy was not afraid; at the back of her mind, though she was hardly aware of it, was the knowledge, like a security blanket, that his mother and sister would be back soon. It was safe to relax and share the pleasure of the kiss.

She had known this would happen as soon as she realized they would be left alone. She could admit to herself now that she had wanted it to happen. Sighing, she wound her arms around his neck and drew him closer. She was half lying against the arm of the couch, and he leaned over her, his chest pressing against her breasts. Suddenly her breasts ached as though with a deep longing. When his hand slid between them to cover one breast, she pressed against it instinctively.

He unbuttoned the front of her dress and slid his hand inside. She felt the heat of it through her lacy bra, and an answering heat was ignited in the pit of her stomach. He pressed open-mouthed kisses against her neck, his tongue delving into the hollow of her throat. She felt giddy and wondered dazedly what that strange, labored sound was. Slowly she realized it was the sound of their breathing. She wondered if she was foolish to feel safe.

"Zach—" Could that reedy, weak sound be her voice? "Zach, we can't . . . they said they'd be back soon."

When his head lifted, his eyes were glazed, the color of a cloudy evening. "They won't come back until the mall closes. They never do."

She stared at him, her body aching for more of his touch and her brain a jumble of contradictory emotions. She was afraid, but all at once fear was not the predominate emotion. She wanted to be loved by this man, she admitted to herself. It would be more than sex, she was convinced of that, because there was more than a sexual attraction between them. He sensed her moods, seemed to understand her feelings as no one else ever had. And she wanted—needed—to explore the unfamiliar terrain through which she knew, some-how, he could lead her. Afterward...she would worry about afterward later.

He rose and, looking down at her, extended his hand. Without hesitation, she took it, and he pulled her to her feet and led her down a hall. When they reached his bedroom, he turned around to gaze at her lovingly. "Don't be afraid of me, Darcy."

"I'm not afraid," she murmured.

His big hands finished undoing the buttons of her dress. He pushed it off her shoulders, and Darcy pulled her arms free of the sleeves as the dress slid to the floor. She stood before him in her bra and half-slip, and his eyes swept over silk and lace and flushed bare skin. He reached around her to unclasp her bra and pull the straps over her arms. She closed her eyes and heard his quick intake of breath. When his fin-gers closed, almost reverently, over her breast, a jolt of pleasure shivered through her.

"Ah, love..." His voice was rough.

She couldn't speak, because her throat was sud-denly too thick to allow the passage of words. But what was there to say? Words could not begin to ex-press the feelings that raced through her.

She opened her eyes and smiled at him. Then she reached out and caught the edge of his sweater and pulled it up. Zach took charge of the job, and with one tug jerked the sweater over his head and tossed it aside. There was a triangular mat of reddish-brown hairs on his chest. Darcy brushed her fingertips down through the chest hair until they touched the bare skin of his belly. He sucked in a breath, and she undid his belt and lowered the zipper.

He felt her sway and clasp his waist to steady herself. Lifting her, he laid her on his bed, deftly divesting her of the remainder of her clothing. Then he peeled off his cords and briefs.

The bed gave with his weight as he joined her. He bent over and looked at her for a long moment. His gaze traveled caressingly down the length of her naked body, the full, ivory breasts with the rosy nipples, the narrow waist, the flare of her hips, the dusky shadow between her thighs.

Darcy felt her nipples harden and grow erect under his long, languid gaze. What she did next stunned her. She lifted her arms and stretched lazily, like a cat preening itself. Then she let her eyes feast boldly on his body as his had been feasting on hers.

His shoulders were broad, his arms and chest rippled with muscle. His waist was narrow, his belly flat, his hips lean, the jut of the hipbones visible beneath the skin. At last, she let her eyes linger at the juncture of his thighs.

Taking her hand, he carried it down and closed her fingers around him. When her hand moved of its own volition, the fingers exploring, caressing, he threw back his head and groaned deep in his throat.

"You're beautiful, Zach," she murmured.

With another deep groan, he came down on top of her, his mouth hotly demanding. Her mouth responded with its own hot demands. He ran his hands slowly over her slim, sleek body, learning its secrets, finding every soft curve and shadowed hollow, touching everywhere.

His fingers feathered over one breast, circling slowly, inexorably, toward the clenched nipple. Restlessly, Darcy squirmed and pressed against his hand. Zach smiled against her mouth and moved down to blow warm, moist breath against her breast. A faint whimper escaped her. Her eyes were closed, her lips parted, her warm breath escaping in erratic puffs. Watching her, Zach slowly drew the pebbled nipple into the hot, wet cave of his mouth. She whimpered again, and he drew on the nipple, suckling gently.

Darcy felt an answering pull deep inside her. "Zach, please," she moaned. Her hands clutched his head. Her fingers clenched convulsively against his skull.

Zach's mouth continued the gentle sucking rhythm that was driving her wild, while his hand smoothed over her concave stomach and trailed down between her thighs.

Her fingers clenched a handful of his hair. Her body felt as if it were on fire. "Zach . . ."

She was in the grip of a frustration she didn't understand. She had never before felt this desperate, scorching need. Its object was hazy but painfully real. The one thing she did understand was that she wanted to wrap her body around his and feel him deep inside her. "I want you," she gasped.

"Yes, love." He trailed his open mouth up her body as he settled over her. He filled her with one long, hard thrust. The pleasure was so intense she thought she would faint. He grew very still, staring down at her, his eyes glazed.

He was inside her and still she wanted something else, something more. What was happening to her? What was this insatiable craving that she had never felt so close to satisfying before? Fretfully, she moved beneath him.

Zach gritted his teeth, held back the explosion until the need shrank to a size he could handle. "There, sweet Darcy," he comforted. "Slow...that's it. We'll get there."

Then one big hand cupped her hips and lifted her. He began to move in her with deliberate slowness, sliding in, withdrawing, sliding in again. At the same time, his thumb stroked the hard little nub exposed by their positions.

For a moment, she moved with him, matching her rhythm to his. Then she could no longer control her body. Fire built in her, a fire that was pure, exquisite pleasure. It was like nothing she had ever experienced. She hadn't even imagined that such pleasure existed. Helplessly, she arched against him, feeling a clustering of sensations at the juncture of her thighs, powerful, explosive sensations, gathering for release.

Suddenly afraid, she whimpered, "No...no."

Zach kissed her damp throat. "Let yourself go, Darcy. Go all the way with me." With her last bit of coherence, she knew that he was asking her to leap into the fire. But she didn't care. She wanted what could be found only at the heart of the flames. She had to have it.

He thrust deep inside her, withdrawing slowly. She let go, and her body arched convulsively. He waited for the convulsion to pass before he slid deep inside her again. A second convulsion racked her, and then another and another. She was totally vulnerable, totally helpless in their grip.

Zach's control slipped, and his rhythm became a wild race to the edge of the world. With a guttural cry, he let it happen.

Chapter 8

Time did not exist. Darcy drifted, like a weightless scrap beyond the pull of gravity. Exhausted, bathed in sweat, she lay beneath Zach's sprawled body, unable to contemplate moving even though his weight was heavy. Gradually she became aware that his head crushed her breast, their legs were tangled together and her hands rested on Zach's buttocks. Tiny aftershocks of pleasure still rippled through her, and she didn't want to move until they stopped.

She was still stunned by what had happened. How could she have lived to the age of twenty-nine—more than a third of her expected life span—without dreaming that she'd missed something glorious? Why didn't people *tell* you these things? She smiled drowsily at the question. Could she describe what she'd just experienced to anyone? Impossible. There were no words...

Zach's body felt like solid lead. But he was crushing Darcy, and he knew it must hurt. He'd try an arm first, and if it moved, then he'd get off her. He lifted his hand and rubbed away the moisture at the corners of his eyes. Tears, he thought, astonished. He hadn't cried since he was a teenager; but Darcy had brought tears to his eyes. He assimilated the knowledge, realizing that he wasn't terribly surprised after all. Somehow he'd known that with Darcy he'd be moved more profoundly than he'd ever been before.

He lifted his heavy head and looked down at her. She lay unmoving, her eyes closed, her kiss-bruised mouth soft and beautiful. He gathered what was left of his strength and eased away. She sighed, the soft sound trembling through her. Her hand drifted up his back.

"Stay," she murmured.

Smiling, he turned on his side and pulled her into his arms. With a soft murmur of pleasure, she snuggled against him. Her eyes remained closed, and her breathing was slow and warm against his neck. She dozed, and for a few moments he let himself pretend that he could hold her like that through the night.

A few minutes later, she stirred. "What time does the mall close?" she inquired sleepily.

"Eight."

Yawning, she rolled onto her back and squinted at her watch. "Zach, it's seven forty-five!" She climbed out of bed and began frantically grabbing articles of clothing and throwing them on.

Zach put his hands behind his head and watched her, amused. She sat on the side of the bed to pull on her shoes. "Zach, get up! They'll be back any minute."

"It takes at least fifteen minutes to drive here from the mall."

She looked around at him, exasperated. "Humor me. Please."

He rolled over on his side and moved his hand in slow circles on her back, as though he just needed to touch her. "Okay." He got out of bed and disappeared into the bathroom.

Darcy ran a comb through her hair and applied lip gloss, using the mirror in Zach's bedroom. She heard the shower going and wandered into the den where she paced, tense and anxious, fearful that Maggie and Linda would return before Zach was dressed again. If so, what would they think? Exactly what you're afraid they'll think, Darcy, she told herself ruefully.

For something to do, she found tea bags and put water in the kettle to boil. At ten after eight, Zach appeared, dressed in the cords and sweater he'd been wearing earlier. Darcy was standing at the kitchen counter, pouring hot water into a cup.

Zach watched her from the doorway. Her expression was one of deep thought. He came up behind her and put his arms around her waist. "Everything all right?"

For an instant she said nothing. "I'm not sure," she muttered finally. "But at least you're dressed. You like to live dangerously, don't you?"

He chuckled. "What's life without a few surprises?"

She smiled in spite of herself. At that moment they heard a car in the drive. Darcy stepped out of Zach's arms. "They're here," she said unnecessarily.

Zach and Darcy were seated innocently in the den with their teacups when Maggie and Linda entered the house. As soon as she reasonably could, Darcy said she needed to go home.

Her preoccupation with her own thoughts on the drive to the hospital worried Zach. Their lovemaking had been fantastic—magnificent. But he still didn't know what she was thinking most of the time. For a few minutes tonight, she'd been totally defenseless and open to him. He'd told himself afterward that he'd made some kind of breakthrough with her, but now she seemed to have withdrawn from him again.

He reached over and took her hand. "You aren't still worrying about Mom and what she might think, are you?"

"No."

"What then?"

She turned her hand over and laced her fingers through his. "I was just thinking, Zach. It's nothing important."

He wanted to say that he needed to know all her thoughts, everything, but he knew better than to get possessive with Darcy. He was sure she would never tolerate any macho bull.

"Have you heard from that guy again? The one who says you're ruining his life?"

"He called Thursday night."

Zach looked at her sharply. He hadn't expected that answer. He'd told himself that the guy was just some

weirdo, making random threats against whoever happened to answer the hot line number that first night.
"He asked for Jo again?"

"Not exactly. I identified myself first and then he
said I knew who he was and that he hadn't forgotten
me, that he was still going to get me."

She drew in a deep breath, trembling a little when
she let it out, communicating her apprehension to him
in a way that mere words could not.

"Have you talked to the police?"

"No—"

"Damn it, Darcy, if you don't report this guy,
I'll—"

"Zach, it's probably nothing to worry about.
Maybe he called the hot line some time in the past and
I took the call. I always identify myself, so that's how
he knows my hot line name. Now he's having a crisis
of some kind, and he's fixated on Jo as the cause of his
problems. As long as he doesn't know my true identity, he can't hurt me." She wanted to believe it, but a
small voice whispered, If it's Bill, he knows exactly
who Jo is.

"I still don't like it. If the hot line's the link— Have
you thought about staying off the hot line for a
while?"

She shook her head. "I don't want to do that unless I absolutely have to. They're always so shorthanded. What I've decided to do from now on is hang
up the instant I know it's him, before he has a chance
to make threats. Maybe that's what turns him on. If I
refuse to listen, he'll stop." But it was oddly comforting, Darcy mused, to have someone concerned about

her. It made her want to offer him something in return.

"Zach, there's something I think I should tell you."
She hesitated, then added all in one breath, "I was married once. It was a long time ago."

Eleven years ago, Zach thought.

"It lasted less than two years."

Zach was surprised, not that she'd been married but that she'd suddenly decided to share something from her past with him. He put his arm around her. "Come here."

She laid her head on his shoulder. "I was somebody else then," she said.

He kissed her hair. "It doesn't matter, but thank you for telling me."

When they arrived at her car, Zach insisted on following her home again. Darcy was glad that he insisted, though she didn't say so. If he knew, he'd realize that she was more worried about the anonymous caller than she would admit. Again, he got out of his car and walked her to her door.

She unlocked it and, turning, found herself being pulled into his arms. He brushed his mouth across her forehead, then claimed her mouth in a kiss that was hot and greedy. Darcy moaned, instantly aroused. She felt weak with the sensuality Zach could call forth so quickly, a sensuality she hadn't known she was capable of before tonight.

When he released her mouth, she leaned her forehead against his shoulder, waiting for her strength to return. Her reluctance to let him go was new, as well. She had always prized her privacy. "I have half a bottle of wine in the refrigerator," she said, after a moment. "Would you like to come in and help me finish it?"

His answer was to reach around her and throw the door open, then walk her backward through the opening and kick it shut with his foot.

There was no further mention of the wine—or anything else. There was only the warm darkness of the apartment, and there were feverish kisses, growing hotter and hungrier as the moments slipped by, and eager hands dealing with buttons and zippers.

At last, there was the scent of clean sheets and bare skin sliding against bare skin. There were caressing hands and mouths and whispered murmurs of wonder and appreciation. There was the fire ignited again in their blood and sweat-slicked bodies writhing, and the loss of control.

Dimly Darcy heard her own long, keening scream and Zach's hoarse cry as together they gave themselves up to the flames.

Long moments passed before Darcy came back to herself. No, she thought dazedly, for hadn't she been truly and fully herself in the moment when she plunged into the fire? Giving herself completely, holding nothing back, becoming one with Zach, an expression that she had never understood the meaning of until now.

But if that were true, then she had been less than herself for twenty-nine long years, until tonight. Not a comfortable thought.

She sighed and caressed the back of Zach's head. He grunted wearily and moved off her, pulling her close to his side. He dragged her leg over his stomach and anchored it with his big hand at her thigh.

"I know you have to get back," she said ruefully.

"Not this minute," he muttered and settled her more comfortably against him.

Darcy pulled a sheet over them, then hugged his hard, muscular body, drowsing in the comfort of his warmth and strength. Within seconds, Zach was asleep, breathing deeply and evenly. She lay motionless, not wanting to disturb him, her mind hovering near the edge of sleep. But she tried not to let it slip over the edge. If they both fell asleep, they might not wake until morning.

Drowsily, she wondered what it would be like to awaken with Zach beside her. It was a surprisingly pleasant thought. Well, they'd passed into new territory tonight, and she knew it would probably happen again. The thought no longer frightened her. She could, she decided, look forward to being with Zach again without relinquishing control of herself and her life. It wasn't so very complicated, after all, or so she told herself.

She did not know the instant when she drifted from her half-waking state into sleep. The harsh ringing of the telephone beside her bed brought her rudely back to consciousness. Mumbling a sleepy protest, she fumbled in the dark for the receiver. She found it finally and snatched it from its cradle just as Zach sat up beside her.

"Hello," she rasped, her throat thick with sleep.

"Darcy..." The hissing whisper was muffled and indistinct, but the venom behind it was unmistakable.

Darcy sat up, dragging the sheet over her as if to protect herself from the hate that was coming over the telephone line. "Who are you? What do you want?"

The terror in her voice drove the clinging remnants of a deep sleep from Zach's mind. He found the light switch and flipped it. Darcy was sitting on the side of the bed, hunched over as though she were trying to get warm.

"Who is this?" Darcy repeated.

"You'll find out. When I'm ready for you to know. I'm coming after you—"

She slammed down the receiver and buried her face in her hands. Zach lifted her to her feet and wrapped his arms around her. She was shaking uncontrollably.

"It was him," she whispered, burrowing her face into his shoulder. "He has my unlisted number. How could he get my unlisted number?"

"Shh." Zach stroked her hair and her back, soothing her. "I'm here. He can't hurt you." With these and other words, he sought to reassure her, over and over. After a while her trembling stopped, and she was quiet in his arms.

"Zach," she whispered, "you didn't give my number to anyone, did you?"

"Of course not."

She sighed. "I didn't really think so."

"I'm going to call the police, Darcy. Do you feel like getting dressed now?"

She nodded wordlessly against his shoulder. He set her away from him and lifted her chin. "It's going to be all right, sweet."

She nodded again and hugged herself. "I'll get dressed," she murmured. She dressed in the living room, where she'd left her clothes. When she took Zach's clothes to him in the bedroom, he was just hanging up the phone. "They're sending an officer over," he said.

"Would you like some coffee? Or a glass of wine?"

"Better make it coffee."

They took the coffee into the living room to wait for the police officer. He arrived twenty minutes later. Zach let him in and made the introductions. The officer's name was Link. He was young—in his early twenties—of average height, sturdily built. He looked like a fresh-faced farm boy.

He declined Darcy's offer of coffee and sat in one of the Queen Anne chairs. He took a small spiral-bound tablet and ballpoint pen from his pocket. "Dr. Shaffer informed us that you've received calls from this man before tonight, Miss Gilbert. But you didn't report it. Why?"

Zach sat beside Darcy on the couch and took her hand in his. Darcy explained to the officer about the hot line. "I didn't think he knew who I was. We don't use our names on the hot line, and the previous times he used my hot line name. I thought he'd picked me because I happened to be the one who answered the hot line the first time he called. But tonight...my home phone number is unlisted. That's what worries me more than anything, that he could get my unlisted number. I've always felt so secure about that..."

"You're sure it was the same man."

Darcy shivered involuntarily. "Absolutely."

"Can you recall the dates of the previous calls?"

"Yes. I work on the hot line on Thursday nights. He called the last two Thursdays soon after I started my shift—about eleven."

"What did he say?"

"Nothing very specific."

"Tell me what you can recall."

"He said I was ruining his life and that he'd make me pay. Tonight he said he was coming after me."

The officer made some notes in his tablet. Zach squeezed her hand reassuringly. She glanced at him with a distracted smile.

"During any of these calls, did you ever think you recognized his voice?"

She hesitated. "No...but he disguises it. The words sound muffled, as if there's something over the mouthpiece."

"Miss Gilbert, do you have any enemies? Anyone you might have had a disagreement with recently or angered in some way?" The officer's gaze drifted over her admiringly. "Maybe it's some guy you used to date, somebody you ditched who didn't want to be ditched."

"No, I don't think it's anything like that. I haven't dated anyone in a long time except for Zach—Dr. Shaffer."

"Hmm." Officer Link made a few more notes, then looked at Darcy and scratched his head. "I don't mean to badger you, Miss Gilbert, but haven't you any suspicion about who it might be? It doesn't seem too likely, after tonight, that this guy chose you at random. He knows you. We can't do much to help you if we don't have a place to start.''

Darcy's fingers tightened around Zach's thumb, though he didn't think she was aware of it. "Well...he's never given a name, and as I said, he disguises his voice..."

The officer watched her closely. "You've thought of someone, haven't you?" he asked. "You'd better tell me.''

"But if I'm wrong..."

"We don't arrest people on somebody else's say-so. I just want to check him out. Lots of times, once these heavy breathers think the police are on to them, they won't even *use* the telephone anymore.''

Darcy expelled a long breath. "Well, I—I did think it might be my ex-husband, Bill Bainbridge.'' She felt Zach's tension through his hand tightening on hers, but she didn't look at him.

Officer Link was writing the name in his tablet. "How long since your divorce?''

"Nine years.''

The young officer looked up. "That's a long time to hold a grudge. Have you heard from him during that time?''

"No.''

"What makes you think it's him?''

"He was living in another state until recently. I ran into him a few weeks ago, and he said he was working here now. He—he asked if I'd go to a movie with him and I said no. I haven't seen him since, but the calls started soon after that.''

"Do you know where he's living?''

"No."

"Well, it'll be no problem to find out, if he has a phone or any utilities in his name. Is there anything else you can tell me?"

She shook her head.

"All right then. You'll be hearing from us, Miss Gilbert."

After she let the officer out, she turned to find Zach standing in the center of the room, studying her thoughtfully. "I wasn't much help to him, was I?" she said.

He came to her and placed his hands on her shoulders.

"Darcy, you tried to play it down, but you're convinced it's your ex-husband, aren't you?"

She raised her shoulders slightly, trying to ease the tension that had gripped them since the phone call. "I suppose I am."

"Why?" he asked gently. "Maybe he didn't want the divorce, but nine years is a long time."

"You'd have to know Bill. He's—well, relentless. He harassed me for months after I left him. I finally had to get a restraining order before he'd leave me alone." She pressed her cheek against his hand as though for comfort. "When I saw him recently, he—he got angry when I said I didn't ever want to see him again."

His fingers kneaded the knotted muscles on either side of her neck. "Sounds like a prize of a fellow. Where did you meet him?"

She bowed her head and remained silent for a moment. "Zach," she said then, "I don't want to talk about this. It has nothing to do with you."

A slap in the face couldn't have hurt him more. What she meant was that it was none of his business. After what they'd shared tonight, he'd thought they had the beginning of a relationship. Perhaps he'd misjudged the situation. He gave an inward sigh and stifled his frustration.

"Then we won't talk about it," he said. "We don't have to talk about anything if you don't want to. Why don't you go to bed now? I'll call Mom and tell her I'm staying for a while."

"No, Zach." She lifted her hand to caress his cheek. "You don't have to stay with me. I'll be all right. I'd really like to be alone now."

With an effort, Zach resisted arguing. She would go so far and no farther, not yet anyway. She wanted him to back off. Although it went against his desire and his better judgment, he did as she asked. He kissed her briefly and let her go. "Good night, sweet. Call me if you need me."

She nodded, but he knew from the look on her face that he shouldn't have added that last suggestion. Obviously she didn't want to need him, or anyone.

Chapter 9

After Zach left, Darcy checked to make sure her purse, containing the Mace canister she'd purchased yesterday, was within easy reach on the nightstand beside her bed. Then she poured herself a glass of wine and phoned the security guard on duty. She explained why the police officer had come to see her and asked him to be particularly watchful when he checked the back courtyard during the night.

She hung up and undressed. She straightened the tangled sheets and plumped the bed pillows against the headboard. Settling back, she cradled the glass of wine in both hands. Tomorrow, she decided, she'd request a new unlisted phone number.

Using the remote control, she turned on the small color television set at the foot of the bed. She ran the channels until she found a comedy movie she'd seen years ago. Scooting down, she pulled the covers up to her waist, feeling somehow comforted by Zach's scent, which still lingered in the bedclothes.

She sipped the wine and watched the antics on the screen. The movie didn't seem as funny as it had the first time she'd seen it, and her mind soon drifted over the evening.

She was still a bit bewildered by the extent to which she'd become involved with Zach in such a short time. Not since her marriage had she allowed a relationship to progress to the place where she now found herself.

It wasn't the sex so much as the deep places where Zach's lovemaking touched her. It had been no real struggle to remain distanced from the other men she'd known, but Zach was the first to stir such a maelstrom of feelings. She now saw that none of the others had been a serious challenge to her emotional defenses.

Perhaps she wasn't as strong as she'd imagined . . .

She didn't want to think about that. For years she had been living her own life, handling her own problems competently. She was astonished by how tempted she had been tonight after that phone call to seek comfort in Zach's arms. It had been difficult to ask him to go. But necessary. She knew her abruptness had hurt him, but she truly hadn't meant to. She simply didn't want Zach trying to solve her problems. She didn't want to start depending on him.

Sighing, she turned off the television set and finished her wine. She wasn't in the habit of leaving a light on at night, but tonight she felt comforted by the soft glow from the adjoining bathroom bulb and left it on. Still, it was a while before she slept.

Random thoughts flitted through her mind in the odd, disconnected manner of nighttime musings. She thought about Claire Champlin and her children, the four of them sharing a single bedroom at the shelter. Were the children starting to rankle at such confinement? It was time she checked on them again.

"How are the children?" Darcy asked Sunday afternoon when she talked to Claire on the telephone.

"They're great. They like having the other children to play with. I don't think they miss being home. The older two didn't even want to talk to their father yesterday on the phone."

"Yesterday? Your husband called you there?"

"Well—no. I called him."

"Oh, Claire..."

"I didn't tell him where we are," she said defensively. "I—I wanted him to know we're okay."

Claire had talked to her husband yesterday, and today she was still at the shelter. That was progress, Darcy told herself. "What was his reaction?"

"Oh, he was real mad at first because I wouldn't tell him where we're staying. He ordered me to come home immediately, but I said I wasn't ready yet. I told him I needed the help I'm getting in my group counseling sessions."

"Good for you."

"He carried on for a while, made threats—but when he saw I really meant it, he broke down and cried. Said he couldn't live without me and the kids. He apologized over and over for what he's put us through."

"And begged for another chance," Darcy finished for her. "You should be well acquainted with the pattern by now."

"I know," Claire said sighing, "but I feel so sorry for him, sitting around the house all alone. He's bound to be drinking a lot."

"He drinks when you're there."

"Yes..."

"Think of the children, Claire. Think about what you'll be taking them back to if you give in before your problems are resolved."

"It'd be the same old story. I've finally accepted it. That's what's keeping me here. Ralph will have to go into counseling himself before things will get better. I just don't know if he'll ever agree to it."

"You can't change him, Claire. The only person you can change is yourself. Concentrate on that. You aren't responsible for his behavior."

Claire laughed mirthlessly. "That's what they tell me in group. I know it's true, but it's so hard to—to let go."

"Every day it will get a little easier." The group sessions at the shelter taught the women to live one day at a time, a guiding principle in most self-help groups. "Call me if there's anything you need, anything I can do for you."

"Thanks, Darcy. You've been a good friend."

Later that afternoon Zach called. "Did you sleep at all?" he asked.

"A few hours."

"No more phone calls?"

"No."

"Mom and Linda left a while ago. Do you want me to come over and give you moral support?"

She smiled, winding the phone cord around her fingers. She knew what would happen if Zach came over, and she needed to get her equilibrium back before she saw him again. "I'm not sure moral support is what I'd call it."

He chuckled.

"I'm fine, Zach, and I wouldn't be good company. I think I'll just curl up with a good book."

"Okay." Disappointment laced his voice. "Talk to you later."

Darcy hung up, aware that she deliberately hadn't mentioned that she would soon have a new phone number. For the time being, she needed some space. Perhaps if the police put a stop to the anonymous phone calls, she'd be in a better frame of mind to deal with Zach.

Darcy did, in fact, sleep well Sunday night. There were no more anonymous phone calls. She arrived at the station Monday afternoon feeling rested and in good spirits.

Unfortunately, her mood was soon to be dampened. She was closeted in an empty office, going over her script for the six o'clock report, when a secretary knocked at the door.

"Come," Darcy called.

"There's a phone call for you," the secretary said. "The same man called a couple of times before you came in. He said to tell you it's Bill. Wouldn't give his last name. He's on two."

Darcy felt an immediate clutch of anxiety in her chest. "Thanks," she murmured, and the secretary withdrew, closing the door behind her.

Darcy stared at the phone on the desk. The second button blinked ominously. Maybe he was no longer satisfied to be only a muffled voice making nebulous threats. Brassy of him to give his first name to the secretary, but then Bill had never been a shrinking violet.

Darcy braced herself and lifted the receiver. "Hello."

His angry voice exploded through the wire. "What the hell are you trying to do to me?"

She swallowed. "I don't know what you mean."

"The hell you don't! I had a visit from the police this morning. My landlord told them where I work, and they came here! They grilled me about some anonymous phone calls you've supposedly been getting. It doesn't take a genius to figure out where they got my name."

"Bill, if you're not the one making those calls—"

"You did give them my name! You told them I was the one!"

"I didn't say you were the one," Darcy interjected. "I said you were the only one I could think of who might want to frighten me."

"I don't believe this! You still want to make me pay, don't you?"

"It's not a matter of—"

"Accusing me of making phone calls I never made! Once you accused *me* of harassing *you*—well, what do you call this?"

"If—"

"What is it with you, Darcy?" he ranted. "What do you want from me?"

"Absolutely nothing, except to be left alone."

"That's what you say, but after nine years, you're still trying to cause trouble for me. You're trying to run me out of town again. It's sick! Do you think you own this city?"

"I'm not trying to run you out of town. I—"

"Well, good, because it's not going to happen. And if the police show up where I work again, I'll sue you for slander! I'll call the newspapers, too. You're such a hotshot celebrity, they'd love to know you're involved in a lawsuit. Two can play at this game!" The receiver banged in Darcy's ear.

She hung up the phone and slumped in her chair. Her heart was beating too rapidly, and goose bumps had popped out on her arms. Amazing. After nine years, Bill's rage could still trigger those old reactions in her. Whatever had been accomplished by the therapy Bill claimed to have undergone, he hadn't learned to control his explosive temper.

He'd sounded the outraged innocent, all right, but she wasn't fooled. She still thought he was making those calls. Who else could it be?

Surely now that he knew he was a suspect, he'd stop. Bill had always had a well-developed sense of self-preservation. He wouldn't risk trouble with the police, she told herself.

The week passed without another anonymous phone call, bolstering Darcy's hope that Bill had been scared off. She requested a new unlisted phone number and received one on Tuesday. She refused to listen to a voice in the back of her mind whispering that if the caller had learned the first number, he could learn the second as well.

As the evenings passed and no call came, she stopped jumping every time the phone in her apartment rang. She hadn't heard from Zach, either. She wondered if he'd tried and discovered the number at the apartment had been changed. But he could call her at the station if he really wanted to talk to her.

By Friday, when she still hadn't heard from Zach, she'd begun to consider calling him to explain about the new number. After all, she had cut him off rather abruptly the last time they talked. She restrained herself, however, fearing that contacting him might lead to a deeper emotional involvement than she could handle at the moment. She still hadn't come to terms with last Saturday night. Was that because she wasn't willing to examine her feelings honestly?

Sunday she almost gave in to her vacillating desire to phone Zach, regardless of the consequences. Instead, though there was a stiff wind, she donned jeans and a heavy sweater and went out for a walk. When she returned to the building, Zach was sitting in the foyer.

He rose as she came through the door. Her eyes flew to his face. His auburn hair was tousled, his skin ruddied by the wind. His blue eyes met hers, and for a long, tense moment they stared at each other.

He wore navy warm-ups and white running shoes. He looked so big in the small foyer, so male. For a moment, she couldn't speak. She just stood there as-similating the warm happiness that rushed through her. How odd that the mere sight of him could cause such a strong reaction.

Until that moment, she hadn't known how very much she'd missed him. "Zach," she managed finally, "I didn't expect you."

"I went out for a run. I didn't know where I was going until I got here." He didn't move, and his gaze never left her face.

She dug her keys out of her jeans pocket. "Come on back." He followed her down the hall. She could feel his gaze on her back. She entered the apartment, tossed the keys on a table and turned to face him. He'd closed the door and was leaning against it.

"It's been a helluva week," he said.

She searched his face, saw the signs of strain around his eyes and mouth. "It's been—long," she said.

"Did you have your number changed to get rid of me?"

"Oh, Zach, of course not."

"You don't have to let me down easy. I'm not fragile. It's the not knowing that's driving me crazy. Just tell me what's going on. If you want me out of here, I'm gone."

"You should know I had the number changed because of those phone calls."

"But you didn't tell me!"

"I almost phoned you several times."

He pushed away from the door and stood with his feet apart. His brows drew together in a frown. "Almost. What stopped you?"

She threw her hands out helplessly. "I wasn't sure what you'd read into it, I suppose."

He narrowed his eyes at her response. The sunlight streaming through a window turned her skin to alabaster. He felt his need rise surprisingly fast. "Why should I read anything into it?"

She took a tentative step toward him. "I don't know. I'm confused, if you haven't guessed that already. But I should have called you, Zach. I'm sorry." She reached for his hand and saw his tensed jaw relax. She drew him into the room. "Let me get you something to drink. Tea? Cola?"

"Water's fine." He followed her into the kitchen.

She dropped ice cubes into a tall glass and filled it at the sink. He drank, watching her intently. He set the glass down. "So," he said.

"So."

The corner of his mouth quirked. "Where do we go from here?"

They were feeling their way toward each other cautiously, she realized, like strangers. She wanted him, even knowing that it was unwise. He wanted her, too, she knew, but he didn't want to risk another rebuff. Her heart softened, and she was suddenly impatient with wisdom and caution. Such recklessness was strange to her, but she didn't stop to think about it.

A gentle smile touched her lips. "I was thinking," she said softly, "it would be nice if you kissed me."

"Come here." The command was quiet and firm. Willingly, Darcy obeyed. His eyes locked on hers—those brilliant, penetrating eyes that conveyed such a range of emotions. Gently he touched her cheek, his thumb angling beneath her chin. A long, shuddering breath escaped her, and her hand rose to cover his.

With the merest pressure of his fingers, he brought her to her toes and firmly covered her mouth. Darcy felt the room sway. His tongue teased the tip of hers, then traced her lips.

"I missed you," he muttered.

Darcy opened her eyes. "I missed you, too." The words were difficult to utter while her gaze was focused on his mouth. Then he was kissing her again, and passion built in her so quickly it made her faint. She realized she was clinging to him.

With a low moan of pleasure Zach buried his mouth against the curve of her throat while his hands ran over her back and buttocks. She felt the bulging hardness of his desire and pressed close to him. Her blood pounded in her head. "Zach," she murmured, "I want you. Love me."

The words were muffled against his mouth as it returned urgently to hers. "I'm sweaty from running," he said raggedly.

Slowly she swam back to reality. "Would you like to borrow my shower?"

His eyes were dark and compelling. "If you'll join me."

"Come on," she said breathlessly and took his hand. In the bathroom, she pulled her sweater over her head and peeled off her jeans. "Hurry," she urged. "I want to see you." An errant thought flitted through her mind: It wasn't like her to be so forward, so eager. But she didn't care.

They stood in the shower, the warm water spraying over them. Her body fitted itself to his. Their passion was too desperate for slow pacing or gentleness. Darcy did not want tenderness, but quick fire and urgent demands. She was stunned by her sharp and insatiable desire for him. What, she wondered dimly, was happening to her?

His hands moved feverishly over her before they cupped her buttocks. He lifted her and entered her with a long, smooth thrust. Swaying, Darcy wrapped her arms and legs around him, letting her full weight rest in his big hands.

"Zach...oh, Zach, yes...yes..."

Eyes closed, she let her head drop back, and his greedy mouth trailed down her water-slicked throat. His tongue tasted the rivulets of water streaming over her. For long moments, he contented himself with ravishing her throat and mouth. Their bodies were locked together, but still.

Heat rushed from the inner core of her outward to her wet skin. Her body tingled everywhere. Whimpering, she squirmed against him, the motion sensual and inviting. With a groan, his hands on her hips clenched reflexively, and he moved in her. Her muscles shuddered then went lax, her joints fluid. Surrender, she thought dazedly. This is what all those love stories mean by surrender.

Paradoxically, in her surrender there was power. He needed her. She could feel it in the urgency of his hands gripping her, taste it in the hunger of his mouth, feel it most of all in the raw rhythm of his thrust.

He tore his mouth from hers and threw his head back, his breath coming in deep, ragged gasps. The rhythm quickly grew wild, desperate, and she clung to him, her face pressed against his shoulder. His body was the only solid thing in the world ruled by sensation.

Her breath forced itself from her lungs and passed through her parted lips in moans and sighs. She raced with him to the summit, holding back nothing, knowing now what was at the top and craving it, needing it.

Release racked their bodies in hot, irresistible waves, overwhelming them with its tumultuous power.

She stood on the mat, her eyes closed, as Zach rubbed her body with a warm, thick towel. When he began to dry her hair, she sighed, and he kissed her parted lips with languid care.

Lifting her, he carried her to her bed, wrapping her tightly in his arms beneath the sheet and quilted coverlet.

She settled her head on his shoulder. She snuggled lazily against him. Contentment wrapped itself around her like a feather bed.

"You're magic," he murmured against her damp hair.

She smiled. "You're the one with the magic wand."

He swatted her bottom playfully through the covers. "Naughty."

She giggled. "I'm serious," she said drowsily. "You make me feel things I didn't—well, I didn't know I could respond to—so thrillingly. I don't know how to explain it.''

His arms tightened around her. ''I understand.'' He was thinking, What kind of jerk had she married who hadn't known she was a sensual woman, capable of profound sexual responses? The guy must have been either abysmally ignorant or so damned selfish he'd assumed sex was all taking and no giving. But if her response was anything like Zach's, it was more than mere sex, too.

He still didn't fully understand his tangled emotions concerning Darcy, but they were strong and myriad. He'd gone through hell last week, thinking she might not want to see him again. He'd decided a dozen times to wait her out, let her contact him if she wanted to see him, and changed his mind a dozen times. He'd been in a pretty bad way when he arrived that afternoon, confused and angry at himself for being so affected.

It had been a long time since he'd felt this helpless and frustrated. His philosophy, worked out during his hectic medical-school days when there was no time for slow wooing, had been: There are dozens of shells on the beach. But Darcy was in a class by herself. He felt himself on the brink of a deeper emotional involvement than he'd ever experienced.

It was obvious that Darcy's feelings were considerably mixed; and the thought that kept nagging at him was that her involvement might turn out to be much less intense than his. He felt like a man on a one-way street, knowing he'd be wise to find out where he was headed before he ran out of exits.

They fell asleep tangled in each other's arms. When they awoke over an hour later, the wind had died. They dressed and went for a ride on rented bikes in the park. On the way back to Darcy's apartment, they picked up a large pizza supreme, canned soft drinks and beer.

They ate in the living room with the television set tuned to a pro football game in which Zach's favorite team was playing.

"I'm stuffed," Darcy groaned, pushing the box containing the last piece of pizza toward Zach. They were sprawled on the couch, the pizza and canned drinks on the coffee table. "Can you finish this?"

With a wry grin, Zach reached for the box. "I'll force myself." The teams were off the field for the half-time ceremonies. He turned the volume down too low to be heard and returned to the couch to finish the pizza. "How many pieces have I eaten?"

"Eight, but who's counting," Darcy said with a laugh.

He pulled her into his arms. "You make me hungry," he murmured as his mouth journeyed over her face.

"Mmm," she sighed and nestled against his chest.

He held her, his chin resting lightly in her hair. The troubling thoughts that had been floating around in his head before he fell asleep were back. He wished he could get inside her mind, read her thoughts, but she remained, in large part, an enigma. Especially when it came to her life before he met her.

"Darcy," he asked finally, "have you heard if the police contacted your ex-husband?"

"They saw him Monday morning," she said unhappily. "Where he works. He called me at the station Monday afternoon. He was so angry. Said I was trying to run him out of town and threatened to sue me."

"Did he deny making the calls?"

"Naturally, but I didn't expect him to admit it."

He was silent for a moment. "He waited until you were at the station to call you. That could mean—"

"That he doesn't know the number here, that he's not the one making the calls," Darcy interjected. "On the other hand, it could mean he doesn't want to call me at home except when he's trying to disguise his identity. He may be detestable, but he's not stupid."

"You sound bitter."

She shrugged. "Maybe I am. I don't like having to deal with him."

He rubbed the back of his hand against her cheek. "Not an amicable divorce, was it?"

"Hardly."

"How soon after you were married did you know you wanted out?"

"Oh, I lived in my fool's paradise for almost a year," she muttered. She pulled a little away from him. "Hard to believe, but I was only eighteen when I married, and living in fantasyland."

He sensed her tension, and his fingers idly worked at the fast-knotting muscles in her shoulders. "Was he seeing another woman?"

"Not that I knew about."

"Then what happened? Why did you decide the marriage was a mistake?"

She sat up very straight then, her back to him. "Don't, Zach, please don't spoil this. I don't want to talk about him."

Abruptly it felt as though a wall of ice had risen between them. She held herself stiffly and stared down at her hands. Zach had never known anyone who could so quickly remove herself from an unpleasant situation, and without even leaving the room. Unfortunately, he wasn't able to compartmentalize his own feelings so neatly, and that disturbed him. He felt baffled, thwarted.

In frustration, he gripped her arms and forced her to face him. "Don't turn away from me, Darcy."

The blood had left her face; she was ashen. She was trembling beneath his hands. Zach was shocked by her extreme reaction. He became aware of his hands gripping her upper arms. He must be holding her more tightly than he'd realized. He instantly let her go.

"I didn't mean to hurt you, Darcy. God, I'm sorry—"

Restlessly she got to her feet and crossed the room. She adjusted a shade and fiddled with the fold in a drapery, as though her fingers had to find something to do.

For an instant, when Zach's hands had gripped her and forced her around, Darcy had been thrown back to her marriage, to Bill's hands touching her in anger, hurting her. She knew it was unreasonable, but knowing didn't stop that flash of feeling.

After a few moments, she'd managed to compose herself and turned around. He was relieved to see color returning to her face.

"You didn't hurt me. I—I guess I'm still on edge about those phone calls."

It was a lie, and he knew it. There was something more than the phone calls behind her reaction. Something she seemed determined to keep from him. Zach decided to be direct. "I have to know where I stand with you."

She looked at him helplessly. "Oh, Zach . . . I don't know."

He got to his feet, walked over to the TV, where the teams were back on the field, and flipped it off. He dragged his fingers through his hair, trying to think how to put his misgivings into words. "I care about you, Darcy," he said haltingly. "But every time I try to get close to you, you push me away."

"I'm sorry . . ."

He expelled a long breath. "I'm not asking for an apology. I just don't want to get in any deeper if this relationship is going nowhere."

Darcy gazed at him, hearing the echo of her own thoughts in his words. He was as fearful as she of getting in too deep. Yet it was happening, they were being pulled inexorably deeper and deeper, every time they were together. But the possibility of not seeing him was even more painful to contemplate.

"I only know I want to see you," she whispered with painful honesty. "Couldn't we go on as we are for now?"

His gaze probed her face. A part of him, the part containing his ego and pride, considered pulling out right then. The rest of him couldn't let her go as long as she wanted to be with him. "Why do you avoid confrontation?"

"Do I?"

His instincts told him that everything that stood between them went back to her marriage. "You know you do."

It was true. She had learned, as a battered wife, to skirt any situation that might lead to confrontation. But she thought she'd worked through all that. She laughed a bit shakily. "I'll work on it, if you'll only be patient with me." All at once her vision was misted by tears. She blinked to clear away the moisture.

Seeing her tears, Zach realized that it wasn't a matter of her willingness to reveal herself to him. It was a matter of capability. For some reason, she was incapable of exposing herself, of becoming that vulnerable. She was terrified of it. His resolve to demand straight answers to his questions wavered.

Going to her, he took her in his arms. "Darcy...sweetheart, I'm sorry." His voice was thick with emotion.

With a shudder of released tension, she pressed against him, seeking comfort. "Oh, Zach." His scent, his touch were no longer those of a stranger, and she craved the familiarity. With a tear sliding down her cheek, she lifted her face for his kiss.

Passions were ignited quickly by soft words and wet kisses and roaming hands. Knowing what waited for her when she and Zach made love, Darcy found herself wanting to return there again and again. She enjoyed and shared and savored. The evening grew late.

Chapter 10

Zach brushed back her hair, now tousled from their lovemaking. They stood just inside Darcy's front door, saying goodbye. They'd been saying goodbye for long minutes now.

"Such a solemn face," Zach murmured and kissed her eyes shut. He thought of the bitterness he had seen in them when he'd questioned her about her marriage, before the shades came down. "I could stay."

She shook her head, then laid her cheek on his shoulder. "No, you need your rest. I don't think you'd get much if you stayed here."

They'd exhausted themselves, making love, but for Zach it was a pleasing exhaustion heavy with contentment. This reluctance to leave her when it was clearly time to go was strange to him. He wanted to sleep with her, wake with her, eat breakfast with her. He wondered if he could be falling in love. "I have Monday and Tuesday off."

"But I don't, and I've a hundred things to do before I'm due at the station tomorrow afternoon." She shook her head again, drawing away. "Oh, I'm sorry. I'm being dishonest. The truth is I have a streak of the recluse in me. I need plenty of time to myself. As a child, I was often alone. I hated it then, but I guess I got used to it. I don't suppose you can understand that."

Zach took her hands in his. "Of course I can. There were times when I was a kid that I'd have given anything to be an only child."

Darcy looked up at him. Her frown cleared. "You're right. All children must sometimes wish they'd been born into a different family. But most manage to grow up without doing something stupid about it."

"Like marrying at eighteen."

Darcy stared at him, her eyes bleak, and Zach drew her close again.

Darcy thought of her excitement in those days before her wedding, of her eagerness to get away from her parent's house. It had never occurred to her that what she was escaping to could be worse than what she was leaving.

Zach thought of the homesickness he'd suffered his first few months away at college. He'd quickly forgotten his complaints about being the only son in a household with three sisters who hogged the bathroom, spilled powder in the sink and left behind dripping panty hose draped over the shower curtain rod and the cloying scent of perfume.

His homesickness had passed, of course, but he'd never stopped looking forward to his visits home. Somehow he doubted that Darcy had ever felt drawn back to her parents' house, even after the breakup of her marriage.

"I could have found another way to leave home," she murmured. "But marriage seemed the answer at the time. I didn't have much imagination, did I?"

"You were too young."

Darcy tilted her head back. "That's what my mother said. She wanted me to wait a year. I accused her of not wanting me to be happy. I couldn't believe she was simply trying to keep me at home a while longer. I thought they'd be glad to be rid of me."

"Your parents must have loved you in their way. Some people aren't comfortable showing emotion."

"I know you're right. But I wanted them to hug me and tell me they loved me." She sighed. "I still feel cheated, and that's silly. They're gone and I'm a grown woman."

"The things we needed as children don't ever leave us completely. If we didn't get those things then, the needs may be even stronger in the adult. If we're lucky, we find other people to satisfy those needs."

Or suppress and deny them, as she had done after her divorce, Darcy thought. Was Zach thinking the same thing? Could he read her that well?

He placed a gentle kiss on her brow and another on her mouth. "Do you like to play golf?"

She wrinkled her nose, thankful he'd decided to let the subject drop. "I played a little in college, but not since then. I've often thought I should take it up again, for the exercise."

"How about Tuesday morning?"

"I warn you, I'll slow you down—way down. I wasn't very good, even in my college days."

"I'll pick you up at seven."

Her brows rose. "In the morning? It's still dark at seven in the morning."

He grinned. "How would you know? You're never up then. It'll be a unique experience. You'll enjoy it. Trust me."

"Seven o'clock," Darcy groaned. "All right—I guess."

He kissed her savoringly. "Good night, Darcy."

"'Night, Zach." She threw the dead bolt and engaged the chain after he had gone. Smiling, she leaned against the door and touched her fingers to her lips where the impression of his mouth lingered.

Monday night, driving home from the station, Darcy noticed a dark sedan about a block behind her. It looked like the car Bill had been driving the first time she saw him after his return to Foleyville. She told herself she was being paranoid. There were hundreds of dark sedans in the city. She took several deep breaths before glancing in her rearview mirror again. The sedan was still there.

Darcy's heart jerked with a rush of adrenaline. She speeded up and took a corner too fast, tires squealing. Gripping the wheel, she slowed for an instant. Then she shot ahead down the deserted street, ignoring the speed limit. The sedan kept pace. She slowed to a crawl. The sedan slowed, too, always staying a block behind her.

For one insane moment, she thought of slamming on her brakes, jumping out and running to confront the driver of the sedan. But then what? Suppose it *was* Bill. Suppose he was as angry as he'd been when he phoned her at the station? There was no telling what he might do.

Calm down, Darcy, she told herself. Calm down and think. There had been no anonymous call since the police had visited Bill. But if they'd succeeded in scaring Bill off, why was he following her?

Maybe Bill hadn't been scared off. Maybe he'd tried to get her new phone number and failed. Maybe he'd waited for her to leave the station tonight in order to follow her and find out where she lived.

She'd call the police.

There was an all-night convenience store a couple of blocks ahead. She drove through an amber light and pulled in at the store. She jumped out and practically ran to the door, turning to look down the street as soon as the glass door swung shut behind her. The sedan went by. She couldn't see the driver. She stood there for several moments, waiting to see if the car would come back.

"May I help you, Miss?"

Darcy whirled around at the sound of the attendant's voice. The balding, middle-aged man was looking at her with a concerned expression.

"I—I want a cup of coffee." Darcy went to the coffee machine and filled a cup, taking it to the counter. She paid for the coffee and returned to her car to drink it. If the sedan came back, she'd call the police, she decided. The coffee was stale and bitter. After two sips, she opened the car door and poured the coffee on the ground.

She waited a full three minutes longer before driving away from the convenience store. She checked her rearview mirror frequently. By the time she reached her apartment building, her heart was beating normally and she was nearly convinced the sedan had not been following her, after all. But if it had, it had stopped when she went into the convenience store.

Still, she left her car and hurried across the parking lot to the building, her key ring with the small Mace canister attached clutched in her hand. The front of the apartment building was well lighted, and she could see the young security guard behind his desk inside.

It felt good to step into the light and warmth of the foyer. "Good evening, Miss Gilbert," the guard greeted her.

"Hi, Percy," Darcy replied absently as she turned to pull the glass door firmly closed behind her. As she did so, a car raced by on the street in front of the building, an unusual occurrence since several twenty-five-mile-per-hour signs were posted. It happened so fast that Darcy didn't get a good look at the car, but she thought it was a dark sedan. She turned to the guard. "Has anyone asked for me this evening?"

"No, ma'am." The guard seemed to study her more closely. "Are you all right?"

"Sure, I'm fine. Good night, Percy." She walked down the hall to her apartment, thinking about the speeding car. She wondered if the sedan she'd noticed earlier had pulled into a dark side street to hide until she left the convenience store, then followed at a

greater distance than before. If so, the driver—Bill—
now knew where she lived.

She shivered as she unlocked her door and stepped
inside. She walked through the apartment, turning on
lights. The apartment appeared to be undisturbed
since she left it that afternoon, not that she had
expected it to be ransacked. But she felt easier after
looking in all the rooms and making sure the windows were locked. She returned to the door and re-
checked the chain and dead bolt.

Only then did she feel secure enough to take off her
jacket and return her keys and the Mace canister to her
purse. She ran hot water in the tub and undressed
quickly. She slid into the water's steamy depths. With
a sigh, she closed her eyes and, scooting farther down,
rested her head on the back of the tub.

You didn't get a good look at that car, Darcy, she
told herself. Only a fleeting glimpse, and she'd been
looking out at the dark street from the lighted foyer.
She couldn't swear it was the same car she'd seen earlier. She couldn't even swear it was dark in color. She
was going to make herself crazy if she didn't stop
imagining the worst.

She felt her taut muscles relaxing, soothed by the
hot water. She was warm and safe in her locked
apartment, and a security guard was on duty in the
foyer.

What she should have done tonight, she told herself, was act on her impulse to jump out of her car, run
back with her Mace canister and demand to know why
the driver of that sedan was following her. At least
then she could've seen if it was Bill. She'd have made

a fool of herself if it had turned out to be a total stranger, but at least she'd know.

Zach was right. She did avoid confrontation, would go to great lengths to do so. It was a holdover from her marriage that she must learn to overcome. If she had gleaned anything from the counseling she'd received after leaving Bill, it was how putting fears and negative feelings into words made them seem more manageable. A few weeks ago, she would have said she'd learned to do that. Evidently old habits were harder to break than she'd realized.

Zach's family had a healthy approach to differences. Everybody spoke his or her mind, and the air was cleared. Darcy wished she could be like that.

People had told her she appeared totally in charge and unflappable on television. It was easy when you were looking into a camera, an inanimate object. The camera distanced you from the world. It wasn't even very difficult to stay distanced when you were with people whose opinion of you was not important, as was the case when she spoke to groups about domestic violence and the hot line. But Zach wanted to get behind her defenses. He made her be herself. Somehow she had begun to want his good opinion of her, almost to need it.

Teetering on the drowsy edge of wakefulness, she thought about the previous day, Zach's hands touching and caressing her, his mouth savoring and demanding by turns, giving and taking, his naked flesh hot against hers, the hard contours of his body fitting so perfectly her soft curves. In the shower, they had been greedy, devouring each other with their passion. Later, the loving had been gentle, slow enough to experience fully every touch and kiss, every nuance of feeling. Darcy had felt like a flower, unfolding slowly, petal by petal, until the very center and core of her were offered up to him like gifts on an altar.

Was this just extraordinary sexual compatibility?

No, she knew what they shared went beyond that. Could she be falling in love with Zach?

Darcy's eyes flew open, and she sat up in the tub. Love. She had not counted on being in love ever again. Love was far too complicated to be worth the emotional trauma.

She shook her head, as though to negate the possibility of love. She liked Zach, of course. She was even quite fond of him. What she loved, she told herself, was making love with him.

Oh, Zach . . .

Aware suddenly that her bathwater had cooled to lukewarm, she climbed out of the tub and got ready for bed. She was, she admitted to herself, looking forward to their golf date tomorrow morning. She wanted to be with Zach. And that was all right, that was fine as long as she knew she could walk away whenever she wanted.

She didn't sleep well and finally got up at five o'clock to brew coffee. Waiting for the morning newspaper to arrive, she made a custard pie and took a package of homemade beef stew from the freezer to thaw for lunch. By the time Zach came for her at seven, the utensils she'd used in making the pie were washed and put away, and Darcy was dressed in gray wool slacks and a matching sweater.

The golf course at the country club where Zach was a member was nearly deserted when they teed off, although several twosomes and foursomes followed them around the course. Most of the golfers were retired people, Zach said, which explained their casual pace. They had all day.

Darcy didn't feel pressured to hurry, and her game wasn't as incompetent as she'd feared. Zach gave her several pointers on her stance and how to hold the rented clubs. She truly enjoyed the outing. Soon the days would be too cold for outdoor activity.

Walking to the pro shop from the eighteenth hole, Zach said, "Would you like to have lunch in the grill?"

"I have beef stew and custard pie waiting at home. There's enough for two."

He looked down at her with a grin. "That sounds even better. When do you have to leave for the station?"

"Two-thirty."

"I don't suppose you could play hooky and keep me company the rest of the day."

"I'd love to," she admitted ruefully, "but I can't."

They had reached the pro shop and he opened the door for her. "Ah, well, we still have three hours." He saw her eyes soften and knew she was thinking, as he was, that there'd be time for lovemaking after lunch. His desire for her seemed insatiable.

She flashed him a mischievous grin as she returned the rented clubs to the rack. "A lot can happen in three hours."

"Indeed," he agreed and maneuvered her into the corner behind the rack of clubs to kiss her. Several golfers were milling around the shop, two of them within three feet of Darcy and Zach, on the other side of the rack. Zach drew away a little to smile at her.

"We'd better go. Those two men over there are watching us."

"And finding us quite entertaining, I'm sure." Zach pulled her toward the door. "Let's get out of here. I want to be alone with you."

He drove the six miles to her apartment too fast. Darcy didn't protest. She was, she discovered, feeling a bit reckless herself.

When they reached the apartment, he pulled her inside and shut the door by pressing her against it. His mouth came down on hers. His teeth scraped against her lips as he groaned and crushed her to him. Her tongue probed his mouth, and her fingers clutched handfuls of his sweater.

After a moment, she pulled her mouth from his and laughed huskily. "If there was a kissing sweepstakes, you'd win hands down, Dr. Shaffer." She sighed and rested her head on his shoulder. With one last hug she pulled out of his arms. "Sometimes I wonder how many other women you're driving wild with your kisses."

He caught her hand and pressed the palm to his lips. "Darcy, do you really think I've wanted to be with anyone else since I met you?"

A fire kindled in the pit of her stomach as she stared up at him. "No, not really." If she believed he was seeing other women, it wouldn't be so difficult to keep her emotional distance. She shook off the anxiety that always accompanied the knowledge that she was already more emotionally involved with Zach than she'd ever meant to be. She said briskly, "I'll heat the stew."

In the kitchen, she emptied the thawed stew into a saucepan and set it on a burner. Zach came up behind her and lifted her hair to kiss her neck. A shivery little laugh escaped Darcy. "If you don't stop that, I'll burn the stew. Why don't you make yourself useful?"

"I thought I was."

She grinned. "Set the table."

He helped himself to another kiss before he did as she asked. Within minutes, they sat down to big, steaming bowls of stew, crisp crackers and generous triangles of custard pie. All at once, Zach was starving and he ate heartily.

"The best beef stew I ever tasted," he announced. "I didn't know you could cook like this."

Darcy titled her head. "I enjoy cooking when there's someone else to cook for. I was thinking of you when I made this last week and put it in the freezer. I thought of you a lot last week."

"Really?"

She nodded. "I was afraid you'd decided to forget about me, that I wasn't worth the trouble."

He looked pleased. "You were? It's nice to know I wasn't the only one who was suffering last week."

Thoughtfully, Darcy finished her stew and cut into her pie. "I think about you while I'm working, too," she said at length. "It breaks my concentration."

"It does?" His grin was delighted. "Well, don't feel lonely. Last week I called one of the nurses Darcy in front of a roomful of doctors. I heard about that for the rest of the day."

She smiled. "Poor Zach. Were you embarrassed?"

"No. Those guys are always razzing somebody." He laid down his fork. "The strange thing is, I've never done anything like that before."

She lifted her shoulders. "I've never had trouble keeping my mind on my work before, either."

"What do you think is going on here?"

"I don't know."

"What are we going to do about it?"

She slid her hand across the table and laced her fingers through his. "You mean ultimately, or right now?"

For answer, Zach stood and dragged her to her feet. The movement was so swift that Darcy gasped, but the sound was swallowed by his mouth. Still kissing her, he walked her backward down the hall to the bedroom. She was breathless with longing by that time. Zach divested her of her clothing so quickly that she hardly had time to draw a breath. His clothes were gone just as quickly. Then he tumbled her onto the bed.

Her hands began to roam over his heated skin, but he gave her no time to explore him. In a single movement, he rolled her on top of him and lifted her to plunge fully inside her.

Darcy cried out, stunned by the need that drove them both, exhilarated by Zach's mindless groans of pleasure. Her mind spun, and her skin felt fevered. Their bodies slid against each other on a film of perspiration.

Darcy cried out again, and her eyes widened as fiery pleasure accelerated, climbing to new heights. Zach's eyes were closed, his face bathed with the sweat of passion. His breathing was ragged, tearing, as he gripped her hips tightly to keep her moving with him.

Then the fire inside her roared out of control, and she could see only hazily, through a mist of exploding colors. She clutched his shoulders to keep from collapsing, but she was falling, tumbling over and over, slowly, losing herself in Zach even as he emptied himself in her.

When Zach returned to reality, he found that he was tangled in the bedclothes, with Darcy in his arms, her face buried in his neck. Now that the fire was ebbing, their damp bodies were beginning to cool. He tugged at the coverlet, succeeding in pulling it over both of them.

"You're wonderful," he murmured, fusing his mouth with hers. "We took care of the immediate problem, at any rate."

Darcy snuggled against him. "Oh, yes." She sighed.

"Do you feel as relaxed as I do?"

"I feel lovely—drunk."

Zach laughed and helped himself to her mouth again.

"Mmm," Darcy whispered drowsily and nuzzled his neck.

She was already half dozing in his arms when he asked gravely, "Do you trust me, Darcy?"

"Of course," she responded without hesitation. "I wouldn't be here with you if I didn't."

"I trust you, too," he said, still very solemn. "To prove it I'm going to tell you a secret."

She stirred, lifted her head and looked at him curiously. His blue eyes caressed her love-flushed face. "When we make love, I feel—I feel everything more deeply than I ever have before. It's never been so magnificent with anyone else."

"Oh, Zach," she said softly and stroked the tousled auburn hair from his forehead. She kissed him tenderly, then snuggled against him once more. "You are very good for me."

Beneath the coverlet, his hand drifted down her back and over her hip. "It's your turn," he said.

"My turn for what?"

His hand made slow circles on her thigh. "Tell me a secret." She was quite still for a long moment, and Zach wondered if she was withdrawing from him again. But he felt no stiffening in her body. She lay in his arms, relaxed, her breath sweet and warm against his shoulder.

For a moment, Darcy held back the words that sprang instantly to mind. How odd, this almost overpowering desire to say what she had never said to her parents, not even to her closest friend.

Perhaps it was because she felt so very defenseless and vulnerable in the drowsy afterglow of lovemaking. Perhaps it was simply that she wanted to give Zach a part of herself that she had withheld from all other people. She did not pause to examine the impulse. She merely gave in to a strong feeling of inevitability. She had to tell him, that was all.

"I was a battered wife," she said.

The words hit Zach like a fist in the gut. Yet, in some part of his mind, hadn't he suspected? How else explain her bitterness toward her ex-husband after nine years? How else explain her defensiveness with him, her obvious fear of emotional involvement?

His arm tightened convulsively around her. "Oh, honey," he whispered into her hair, "I'm so sorry... I'd like to kill him."

"It only happened three times...the first two times I wanted to believe his promises that he'd never hit me again. The third time, I knew it would happen again—it would go on happening."

"Ah, love..."

Once she'd revealed her dark secret, the need to continue talking was overwhelming. She wanted Zach to know the kind of person she'd been then. She wanted him to understand.

"Looking back on it, I'm amazed that I knew it wouldn't stop. I wasn't even twenty yet, but I had a strong conviction, and I didn't doubt for a second. Where it came from, I don't know. I talk to so many battered women who can't accept that it's never going to stop as long as they stay in the relationship. They go on for years and years, refusing to accept it."

He stroked her back as though he were comforting a child. "Many nineteen-year-old women wouldn't have been strong enough to leave, even knowing what their life would be like if they stayed." He kissed her shoulder and held her close.

"It's strange, but the hardest thing was to admit that I'd judged so poorly when I married him. I knew he would beat me again if I stayed, and he'd killed whatever love I had for him, but it still wasn't easy to leave him."

He combed his fingers through the silky strands of her hair and pressed her head against his shoulder. "I'm not sure I understand that."

She sighed. "For one thing I was terrified of what he'd do. He made such wild threats. And I had no means of support. I wanted to go to college, but I had no money and I would have died before I asked my parents for help. I didn't want them to know he'd hit me."

"Pride," he said gently.

"Or stubbornness. I tried to get a job and couldn't at first. Finally, I went to work, waiting tables five evenings a week. The job's only virtue was that it left my days free, so I enrolled in college. I carried a full load, went all year round and finished in three years."

"Sounds like a grueling three years."

"It was, but I knew it wouldn't go on forever. That made it bearable."

He continued to stroke her comfortingly.

"At first," she said after a moment, "Bill came around all the time, to my apartment and to the restaurant where I worked, begging me to come back or threatening to kill himself or me or both of us. I had to get a restraining order." Her voice shook and she broke off.

"You don't have to say any more."

"No, I want to." She swallowed. "After the police suggested he leave town, I at least didn't have him to contend with anymore. And I got counseling. But there were still times when I wanted to give up. There were days when I just didn't think I could keep going. But then I'd think about waiting tables for the rest of my life, and that spurred me to give it one more week, and then one more month."

Listening to her, imagining a man, any man, hitting Darcy, Zach felt fiery anger balling in the pit of his stomach. For the first time in his life, he was almost ashamed of being a man. "If he ever bothers you again, I want you to tell me."

Darcy heard the fury behind the words. She tilted her head and kissed his clenched jaw. "You don't need to fight my battles for me. Besides, my life in those days wasn't all grim and hopeless. I loved my college classes, even though I was sometimes so tired I fell asleep during lectures. I also liked the satisfaction I got from taking control of my life, setting goals and reaching them. Maybe that's why I have such a thing about being my own person."

"I can understand that," Zach said. He also understood better what he was up against. As a result of what she went through with her ex-husband, Darcy shied away from commitment. To her, commitment meant relinquishing control. On the other hand, she had trusted him enough to share the dark, humiliating parts of her past with him. That was a step in the right direction, he told himself.

They were both silent for a few moments. At length, Darcy said, "I've never talked to anyone about this except my counselor. I never thought I'd want to."

"Thank you," he said simply. "That means a lot to me."

"You make me forget myself," she said. "You make me forget everything except—oh, Zach, I've forgotten the time, too." She lifted her arm to peer at her watch. "Thirty minutes—I have thirty minutes to get to work!" She scrambled out of bed.

He lay there, watching her pull clothes from the closet and throw them on, regretting that the sharing of confidences was over. She was intent on other things now, and he felt almost jealous.

Sighing, he got out of bed and dressed. "I'll clean up the kitchen," he said, standing in the open bathroom door. Darcy was at the bathroom mirror, dealing with her hair and makeup. He wanted to tell her how it hurt him to think of any man abusing her. He wanted to continue comforting her, reassuring her. But she wouldn't accept it now. The moment had passed.

"I'll lock up when I leave."

"You don't have to bother with the kitchen."

"I want to."

She tugged a wayward strand of hair into place and picked up a can of hair spray. "I look like I just got out of bed," she muttered.

"Exactly the way I like you," he said, eliciting a smile from her. "Don't worry. You look beautiful, as always."

She gave him a glance and her smile broadened. "As I said, you are good for me, Dr. Shaffer."

Chapter 11

The next Saturday afternoon, Darcy sat in one of the folding chairs arranged in two rows in the big sitting room at Hope House. She was there for Claire Champlin's "first step" ceremony to celebrate the completion of four weeks in the shelter's group counseling program. Two other women were being similarly honored. The three sat on the couch, wearing their best clothes, carnation corsages presented by the housemother pinned to their dresses.

The window near Darcy looked out on the dead grass of a yard, where a tricycle lay on its side. The sky was gray and hazy. November had been ushered in with forecasts of impending sleet and snow. It was still very early for snow in the region, but it wasn't unheard of in November.

The first winter storm hadn't materialized. The storm had passed farther north than expected. But a second sleet-snow forecast had been issued that morning. Gazing at the sky, Darcy reflected that the forecast might become reality this time.

The atmosphere inside the house was sunnier. The three honorees beamed with pleasure as Dr. Ferguson, the shelter's psychologist and group leader, praised them for the progress they'd made in four weeks. Unaccustomed to praise, the women basked in it.

Claire looked like a younger version of the woman Darcy had seen when she took her to the trauma center with a broken arm. Her blond hair, shining with cleanliness, was arranged around her face in an attractive frame of curls, and her dress matched the rosy glow in her cheeks.

"It's taken courage and determination to reach this point," the psychologist was saying, "and I congratulate you for it. We've talked about this in group, and I know all of you realize you've completed only the first step in your recovery. I know you're all planning to continue in counseling and are beginning to make other good decisions for yourselves. I'm proud of you. Now, before we have our refreshments, I want to give each of you the opportunity to say whatever is in your heart."

When it was Claire's turn to speak, she looked out over the small audience, her gaze picking out Darcy. "I want to thank Dr. Ferguson and the housemother and the other women in my group for their support and understanding. Most of all, I want to thank Darcy Gilbert who I first talked to on the DV hot line. She's been a real friend. Without her encouragement, I wouldn't be here."

Smiling, Darcy discovered that she had to swallow a lump that had lodged in her throat. To most people, completing four weeks at Hope House probably wouldn't seem an uncommon accomplishment. Darcy knew better; she knew these women had arrived at the shelter defeated and helpless, their self-images stomped into the mire of violence and guilt. You had to have been through it to understand how far they'd come in four weeks, and how far they still had to go.

A few minutes later, Claire joined Darcy at the refreshment table. Darcy hugged her and they accepted cake and punch from a shelter resident who was serving. Carrying the refreshments, they made their way to two chairs in a corner. "I have something for you," Darcy said, bringing out the gift-wrapped box she'd tucked behind the chair when she arrived.

Claire's eyes held a sparkle, so different from the flat look of hopelessness that had been there when Darcy met her. "Oh, you shouldn't have." Claire set down her plate and cup and, laughing, reached for the box. "But I'm glad you did."

Claire's laugh was a light, tinkling sound. Darcy reflected that Claire was laughing more these days. She tore into the wrapping as eagerly as a child. Lifting the soft blue cotton sweater from the box, she squealed with delight. "It's beautiful!" She held it against her breast. "Blue's my favorite color. Oh, I love it." She reached out to squeeze Darcy's hand. "Thank you, Darcy."

Darcy returned the pressure of Claire's fingers. "You've earned it and more. I know the past four weeks haven't been easy for you, but you came through. You even look like a different woman."

"I feel like one—some of the time." She folded the sweater into its box. "Other times, when I think about where I am and what I'm doing, I get a panicky feeling in my chest. I wonder what ever made me think I could do this, and I want to run home as fast as I can."

"I know. You'll get over that. Before long that feeling will go away for good."

Claire looked at her solemnly. "Promise?"

"I swear it. Now, tell me your plans."

"The kids and I are going to stay here while I look for a job."

"Where are the children, by the way?"

Claire picked up her cake and punch. "My mother took them for the day. I love them, but I need a day away from them once in a while."

Darcy eyed her thoughtfully. "I'm sure every mother feels that way. It's nothing to feel guilty about."

Claire laughed. "You know me, don't you? Old Claire has to be responsible for everybody close to her, every hour of the day. Otherwise, I'm shirking my duty."

"Don't give me that. You wouldn't know how to shirk."

"It's hard to get rid of those old feelings, though." She took a bite of cake.

"One day—"

"At a time," Claire finished for her.

"Right. So, tell me, what sort of job are you looking for?"

"Anything. I used to be a good typist, but most office jobs now require computer skills. I want to take a course at the votech school as soon as the kids and I get settled in our own place. In the meantime, I'll take any job I can get. I'll probably end up clerking in a department store at first, but that's all right.''

Darcy was pleased to hear that Claire was making definite plans for the future. ''You're not going back to Ralph, then?''

Claire's eyes were sad as she shook her head. ''He still refuses to get counseling.''

''So you're in contact with him.''

''I call him once a week to let him know the kids are all right. He keeps trying to find out where we're staying, but I won't weaken.'' Her expression remained clouded for an instant. ''Frankly, I worry about what he'll do if he does find us.''

''You can always get a restraining order,'' Darcy said. ''That's what I had to do.''

Claire looked at her sharply. ''Did your husband leave you alone after that?''

''Yes. In fact, he left town.'' If only he'd stayed away, she added to herself, but she wouldn't mention the disturbing events that had transpired since Bill's return. Claire had too many problems of her own.

Claire sighed. ''I hope I don't have to do that. After all, Ralph is my children's father.''

''I know that complicates your situation,'' Darcy said. ''But it'll work out, Claire. I made a life for myself after an abusive marriage, and you can, too. You know you can call me any time you want to talk.''

Claire smiled bleakly. ''Thanks—oh, and would you mind giving me your home phone number again? I seem to have lost it.''

"I'm glad you reminded me—I have a new number. I'll write it down before I leave."

"Knowing you and seeing what you've accomplished gives me a lot of encouragement. I really don't know what I'd have done without you."

"You'd have found the strength in yourself," Darcy assured her.

It was after five when Darcy left Hope House, and she had to make several stops before going home. Zach was picking her up at seven-thirty for a movie and a late supper.

They spoke on the telephone almost every day now, unless they had plans to see each other. Zach knew the best times to call her at the station and that she rarely went to bed weeknights before midnight. She had his work schedule on her refrigerator door; he was working days this week.

They did not talk of the future. Zach had learned that too much talk of tomorrows made Darcy uncomfortable. That she had spoken to him of her past, though briefly, reassured him. He hoped it was a bigger step than Darcy realized.

Darcy needed time. Time to adjust to sharing a part of her life with someone. Time to find out if what was between them would develop naturally into something stronger, or if she would come to feel threatened by it. The advice she had given Claire applied to her own case: one day at a time. She didn't want to get ahead of herself. The future would be there, if there was to be a future for her and Zach together.

She was honest enough to realize that even admitting the potential for a future with Zach was a step into

unfamiliar territory, a step she had never made with
anyone since her divorce.

She was changing in other ways, too. She continued to think of Zach more often than was prudent.
What was he doing at that moment? Was he thinking
of her? If she concentrated hard enough, would her
thoughts fly through the air to him and tell him that he
was on her mind?

Fanciful thoughts for a woman who'd not known
she had a propensity for the fanciful. The past month,
she'd repeatedly surprised herself. There were times,
she had to admit, when she almost believed Zach was
an enchanter who'd cast a spell over her.

What's happening to you, Darcy? she asked herself. But she had no answer yet. She was in no hurry
to seek one. For now, she found it a refreshing change
to float along, taking each moment as it came, savoring it and trying to make it last. She might continue to
find it refreshing, or she might not. She was content
to wait and see.

By six-thirty, she'd finished her errands and she
drove home. Taking her usual space in the apartment
parking lot, she left her car, carrying clothes on hangers from the cleaners in one hand, bundles from the
drugstore and supermarket in the other.

Thinking about what she wanted to wear that night,
she reached the entry door and peered inside, hoping
to catch the security guard's eye so she wouldn't have
to put down her bundles to find her key.

The guard was slumped down in his chair behind the
desk, feet up, head back, eyes closed. Sighing, Darcy
set down her packages and fished her key ring out of

her purse. The guard woke and sat up, embarrassed, as she pushed open the foyer door.

"Catching a nap, are we, Percy?" Darcy teased.

"Can't seem to help myself," the young man admitted. "The baby's teething. My wife and I were up and down all night. Guess I better make a pot of coffee. You gonna tell the manager you caught me sleeping?"

"My lips are sealed."

He breathed a sigh of relief. "Thanks, Miss Gilbert."

"Don't mention it, Percy. Do you think you could carry these bundles for me? I need a free hand to unlock my door."

He jumped up. "You bet, Miss Gilbert. Here, give me those clothes, too."

As he followed her down the hall, Darcy said, "I'm expecting Dr. Shaffer at seven-thirty, so you can send him on back."

"Yes, ma'am."

As she approached her apartment, Darcy noticed a small triangle of white extending from beneath the door. She bent to pull out a square envelope. Turning it over curiously, she saw that there was no writing on the envelope. "This wasn't here when I left at one," she said. "Have you let anyone in this afternoon?"

"Just the Daileys' housekeeper and Mr. Vandever's mother."

Frowning, Darcy ran her fingernail beneath the envelope flap and drew out a folded sheet of paper. The note was printed with a pencil in square block characters such as a child just learning his letters might make.

I'm watching you. You can't hide from me. I can get to you any time, day or night.

There was no signature.

Fear turned Darcy's blood to ice water. Her hands shook as she replaced the note in the envelope. "Somebody else got in here, Percy."

The young man looked profoundly worried. "That's impossible."

"Perhaps while you were patrolling outside . . ."

"But I always leave the foyer door locked, and I'm never away from the desk longer than fifteen or twenty minutes."

Plenty of time for someone to get in and out without being seen, Darcy thought. "I'm going to turn this note over to the police, Percy. They may want to talk to you."

"I'll be glad to talk to them," he said, a bit defensively, Darcy thought. "I got nothing to hide."

"I wasn't implying that you do," Darcy assured him as she took the clothes and bundles from his hands.

The apartment seemed cold and Darcy turned up the heat before going to the phone to call the police station. She explained about the note and mentioned the threatening phone calls. The woman who took Darcy's call asked for the name of the officer who'd taken her complaint about the phone calls.

"Officer Link."

"Let me check and see if he's working today." The woman came back after a few moments. "He's on duty. I'll get word to him. He should be at your place soon."

"Thank you." Darcy replaced the receiver and hugged herself, wondering why the apartment wasn't warming up. When she looked at the temperature gauge, the reading was seventy-two. The chill was coming from inside her.

Zach would be there in less than an hour, and she hadn't even started to get ready. But the thought of going out was no longer appealing. She felt safer in her apartment, even though she knew the feeling wasn't entirely reasonable. After all, he'd gotten past the security guard once. What was to keep him from doing it again?

She went back to the phone and dialed Zach's number. It rang five times before he answered. "I was in the shower," he explained. "Couldn't wait till seven-thirty to hear the sound of my voice, eh?"

"I needed to hear your voice, Zach, but that's not the only reason I called." It was true, Darcy realized, the mere sound of Zach's voice gave her a feeling of security. "Would you mind terribly if we don't go out tonight? Something unpleasant has happened—"

"What?" he asked, instantly alarmed. "Did you get another threatening phone call?"

"It was a note this time. Somehow he got into the building and slipped it under my door."

"Call the police. I'll be right over."

"I've already called them. And—thanks, Zach."

Officer Link arrived ten minutes later, accompanied by an older officer named Wilasky, a stout man with a military bearing. His steel-gray hair was clipped so short his scalp shone through.

Wilasky took the note, scanned it briefly and handed it to Link. "Cheap stationery," he said. "You can buy it almost anywhere."

After reading the note, Link said, "We'd like to take this with us, Miss Gilbert."

She nodded, and Link took out his spiral tablet and pen. "When did you find it?"

"When I came home. About six-forty."

"You're sure it wasn't there when you left earlier?"

"Positive."

"How long were you gone?"

"Since one this afternoon. I went to a party for a friend. After that, I ran errands."

Wilasky rose abruptly. "I'll go talk to the security guard and check out the building." He let himself out while the younger officer continued to question Darcy.

Wilasky was back a few minutes later. While Darcy and Link talked, he strolled around the apartment, examining doors and windows. He came back to the living room as Officer Link was closing his tablet. "Guard says he only left the lobby twice to go out and check the courtyard and exit doors. Says he left the lobby door locked and he saw nothing suspicious outside. Came on duty at four. I got the name and phone number of the guard he relieved. I'll try to talk to him tonight, Miss Gilbert."

Darcy hesitated before she said, "Percy was asleep when I got home. I had my hands full and tried to get his attention so he could open the foyer door for me, but I couldn't wake him." She looked from Link to the older man. "I'm not accusing Percy of dereliction of duty. I know how boring it must be, sitting in that lobby for eight hours at a stretch, and he told me he was up with the baby last night. I know the lobby door was locked when I returned because I had to put down my parcels and get out my key."

"There's not a lock made that can't be opened without a key," Wilasky said.

"Somebody who knows locks—it'd take him less than a minute to get in," said Link. "He could do it with the guard asleep right there in the lobby and not wake him."

"More likely he did it when the guard was outside," Wilasky said.

"We'll talk to your ex-husband again, Miss Gilbert," Link said, "but that's all we can do. You've given us no proof that he's behind this little campaign, and this—" He held out the note. "We won't be able to match this with his normal handwriting. We can ask him to print something for us, but he can refuse and there's not a thing we can do about it. In fact, he was pretty irate when we talked to him at his place of business. He may refuse to talk to us again."

"He phoned me after you questioned him," Darcy said. "He said he'd sue me if I sent you there again."

"You aren't sending us," Link said. "He's bluffing, anyway."

"You've got pretty good locks in this place," Wilasky muttered, "better security all around than most buildings. But you might want to think about having an alarm system installed."

"Yes, I will. Thank you for coming by."

Darcy let them out. Zach passed the police officers in the hallway. He was carrying a large grocery sack, which he set down in the nearest chair.

"I brought a couple of steaks. I'm going to cook for you." He took her chin between his fingers and studied her drawn face. "Are you all right?"

Wrapping her arms around his waist, she pressed her cheek against his chest, seeking the comfort of his arms. "I'm fine, now that you're here."

He held her close and felt her shiver. "What did the note say?"

She told him. The words were etched in her brain. "He printed it with block letters, so they can't match it with his handwriting."

"You still think it's your ex-husband?"

"I don't know anyone else who hates me enough to do these things. The police will question him again, but he doesn't have to talk to them if he doesn't want to. *I'm* sure Bill's doing this, but there's no real proof."

Zach uttered an oath. "How did he get into the building?"

"Apparently it's not very difficult to pick a lock, if you know how. He could have come in while the guard was outside for a few minutes."

He cupped her face in his hands and kissed her with great tenderness. "I think you could use a drink. I brought a bottle of champagne."

"Sounds lovely. I'll get the glasses."

In the kitchen, Zach emptied the sack—two thick filets, fresh salad vegetables and a quart of rum-raisin ice cream. Darcy poured the champagne and touched her glass to Zach's. "To your many talents, Dr. Shaffer," she said with a smile. She was, she realized, quite hungry.

He kissed the tip of her nose before taking a sip of champagne. "Name one."

"I can do better than that." She took a swallow of the bubbly wine. "You know how to make a woman feel cherished. You're a great kisser, not to mention your other—um, skills in the lovemaking department. You can cook . . ."

He snagged her waist and drew her against him to claim her lips in a lingering kiss that tasted of champagne. "You taste good, too," Darcy murmured against his lips.

He lifted his head reluctantly. "I'd better attend to dinner first, and then . . ." He gave her a wicked smile.

Her eyes lit up. "I think I'll have a shower while you do that." She left, taking her champagne with her.

As it turned out, Zach was an accomplished cook and dinner was better than anything they could have eaten in most of the restaurants around town. The threatening note forgotten for the moment, Darcy ate heartily.

Zach's appetite for food was distracted by an appetite of another sort. Darcy, rosy and fresh from the shower, wore nothing but a white terry robe and something that smelled like lilacs. Throughout the meal, his eyes kept straying to the dewy, shadowed cleavage where her robe lapped in front.

Whenever she caught him looking at her, she gave him a dreamy smile and lowered her lashes provocatively. She knew what she was doing to him and she was enjoying it. When she finished her steak, she rose from her chair. "I'll make coffee to go with dessert."

"The hell you will." He pulled her into his lap and found her mouth. Tasting the raw need that matched her own, she began unbuttoning his shirt.

"Don't you want dessert?" she inquired as his lips moved to her neck.

"That's what I'm having." He reached inside her robe and found her breast, groaning as his hand took possession. "God, you drive me crazy, woman! Let's go to bed."

"Yes," she murmured even as he rose, sweeping her into his arms.

Light from the living room provided twilight illumination in the bedroom. Darcy slipped out of her robe and watched from the bed as Zach quickly divested himself of his clothing. His body blended into the shadows, but she remembered every line and angle and she knew that he was beautiful.

He trembled as he lay on top of her. His heartbeat was thunder in his ears. His breath was ragged. With a smile or a look, she could destroy his control. No one before her had ever had such a devastating effect on him. There was some satisfaction in knowing that he could make her lose control, as well.

He stared down at her, and she lifted a hand to brush the hair from his forehead. Her fingers shook. "Why can't I get enough of you?" she murmured. "I only have to look at you to want you. It scares me."

"You have the same effect on me. There's nothing to be scared of."

"Isn't there?" She gazed up at him. "I'm not so sure."

Tenderly, he kissed her eyes closed. "Don't worry about it. Tonight we're here, just you and me. We can forget everything else and take our fill of each other."

She cradled his head in her hands, and their mouths fused, and the world dropped away. The kiss was intense with emotion. For long minutes, Darcy only wanted him to kiss her endlessly. They made soft, murmuring sounds as their lips parted and met again and again. Hot, intoxicating, so sweet it was almost painful. He stroked her shoulder and the side of her breast while the kiss went on and on. She wanted him to keep kissing her until the world ended.

His hands roamed farther, touching her with exquisite gentleness, while his mouth remained on hers. She released his head to grip his shoulders, her nails digging into his flesh as the need for more than kisses began to build in her.

When the tips of his fingers traced her inner thigh, her legs parted for him. He continued to caress the silken texture of her thighs, briefly passing over the soft mound at their juncture. He felt her tremble.

All the while, he feasted on her mouth, using his lips and his teeth and his tongue. She murmured his name over and over, thrilling him. When they made love, she was his totally, and he wanted to savor her. His hands explored the sweep of her hips, the curve of her waist, a taut nipple, her satin smooth arms. She murmured words he couldn't understand. She was nearly delirious with wanting him.

He couldn't wait any longer. He slipped inside her, and she moaned. Still savoring the taste of her mouth, he took her slowly, letting her need build, moment by moment, forcing back his own explosive passion until he could no longer deny it.

At the very instant when she cried out with the final rush of pleasure, he lost himself in her. Darcy, he thought dizzily...after you, how can there ever be anyone else?

Chapter 12

Two hours later Darcy dipped rum-raisin ice cream into bowls. She was dressed once more in the white terry robe and furry white mules. The apartment was warm and cozy with the odor of wood smoke from the fire Zach had built in the living-room fireplace.

"I'm glad we didn't go out," she said, turning to watch him pour coffee into their cups. He'd put on pants and shirt, leaving the collar open, and was in stocking feet. She thought idly that it would be nice to have a man's robe at her place for him to use. Then she wondered where such a domestic thought had come from and shook it off.

"It makes me feel special to have you cook for me."

"You *are* special."

"It was a lovely meal."

"Particularly the bedroom intermission."

Darcy went to stand behind him, slipping her arms around his waist. "That's true." With a sigh she rested her cheek on his back. She felt utterly contented and safe. Nobody but Zach could have accomplished that tonight, after she'd found that anonymous note. "Next time, I'll cook."

"Tomorrow evening?"

Standing on tiptoe, she nipped an earlobe playfully. "You might at least argue with me, offer to take me out—somewhere expensive, since we didn't go out tonight," she teased and slipped her hands under his shirt to trail her fingers up his chest. She felt a ripple of response.

"What makes you think I planned to take you to a pricey joint tonight? I had in mind Maxie's Diner."

"What a classy guy." She ran her hands over his shoulders. "I'm not sure I can compete with Maxie, but I'll give it my best shot tomorrow night."

Amused, he turned and gathered her into his arms.

"At my place," he said.

"If you insist."

He kissed her nose. "I do. What's on the menu?"

"In the way of food, you mean?"

He grinned. "Yeah."

Smiling, she cocked her head. "I haven't decided. I'll surprise you."

"Good." He twined a lock of her hair around his finger. "I like it when you surprise me."

"Have I done it often?"

"Every time we make love."

She pressed her face to his chest and clung to him. "Explain, please."

He put his hand under her chin and lifted it. Her eyes were soft and glowing. "Each time it seems new, like the first time."

"Does it, really?"

"Oh, yes. You make me feel powerful and helpless all at the same time. Even when I've reached the point of physical impossibility, I want to experience it again to see if the magic's still there. It always is."

"I know." She nodded gravely. "It's the same for me."

He smiled, brushing a finger over her lips. "It's comforting to know we're victims of a mutual insanity."

"Going mad together, are we?"

"Or saner than we've ever been."

"Interesting. I thought doctors only thought about practical things."

"I hate to disillusion you, but doctors are mere mortal men. I never feel that more than when I'm with you." He set her away from him. "That's quite enough philosophy for one night. Our ice cream is melting."

They carried the food to the living room where they settled on the floor in front of the hearth. The wood fire provided the only light in the room. Zach leaned against the front of the couch, and Darcy sat between his outstretched legs, her back resting on his chest, her head on his shoulder.

He spooned melting ice cream. "I want to make a suggestion." He pressed his lips to her temple. "But I don't want you to take it the wrong way. I'm not trying to arrange your life or anything like that."

She quirked a brow. "What is it?"

"I want you to move in with me." She grew very still against him. He added, "Just until the police catch this guy who's harassing you."

"What if they don't catch him?" she inquired carefully. "The way it's going, they're not likely to."

"We can't cross that bridge till we reach it."

She sighed.

"So, what do you think?"

"I couldn't possibly, Zach."

"How did I know you were going to say that?" he asked in exasperation. "At least, consider moving to a motel for a few days."

She took a bite of ice cream and chased it with hot coffee, savoring the combination of tastes. "I won't be driven from my home."

"Prudence is not the same thing as cowardice," he said mildly.

"I'd feel less safe in a motel. I chose this apartment building because of the security."

"The same security that failed today," he reminded her.

"I'm sure the guards will be more alert, now that he's managed to get by them. They'll be determined not to let him show them up again."

"What if he's even more determined than the guards? You told me once that your ex-husband can be relentless."

"He's only trying to frighten me," Darcy insisted. "He won't carry it any farther than that."

"How can you be sure?"

"Don't you see, he thought I'd give him another chance after he'd had counseling. But I told him to stay out of my life. I insulted his male ego, so he wants to make me squirm.''

Zach shook his head. ''I'm not convinced it's that simple.''

''If I move out of my apartment, even for a few days, he'll know he's succeeded. I won't give him that satisfaction.''

''All right.'' He set his empty bowl aside and finished his coffee. ''I know better than to argue with you when you've made up your mind.''

''You mean I'm opinionated.''

''I couldn't have put it better myself.'' He nuzzled her neck.

She disposed of her bowl and cup and turned in his arms to look into his eyes. ''Nobody's perfect.'' His expression told her that, in his eyes, she was as close as human beings came. A very prejudiced opinion, of course, but it was lovely to know he held it. All at once, it seemed as though they had not yet made love that evening. She hungered for him.

With a single accord, they reached for each other. He kissed her gently. Their pace was slow and dreamlike as they pleasured each other. The flickering firelight turned the room into an enchanted place.

The fire gilded their bodies. Darcy's hair was a dark mist falling over her shoulders. Her skin was pale. But her eyes were dark, twin flames of fire reflected in their centers. Zach worshiped her with his body.

The smell of wood smoke mingled headily with the clean, soapy scent of her skin. She smiled up at him, and the flickering light caught her glistening tears.

''Each time is more beautiful than the last,'' she whispered.

* * *

Darcy had just finished breakfast at eleven the next morning when the guard in the lobby rang to say that Officer Link was there to see her. She'd slept lightly, awakened several times during the night by the wind or faint settling noises in the building that ordinarily didn't disturb her. At one point, about three o'clock, she'd turned on the light and read until she felt sleepy again. For a few moments, she'd even given serious consideration to Zach's suggestion that she move out for a few days. Not to Zach's place—she still wasn't willing to make what seemed to her a commitment, even if the arrangement was temporary—but to a motel.

Dawn shed common sense on her nighttime fears. What she'd told Zach about not wanting to be run out of her home was true. Further, moving wouldn't solve her problem. She had to go to work five days a week and continue with her life. She couldn't hide from someone who was determined to find her.

Her doorbell rang as she was pulling on warm-ups and her white mules. She went to admit the officer.

He stepped inside and took the chair she offered. "I was in the neighborhood, so I took a chance you'd be here."

"I'm embarrassed to interrupt your Sunday. It could have waited until tomorrow."

"I'd forgotten it was Sunday," he said, shrugging. "I've been on duty all weekend."

"I'm glad I'm not taking you away from your family."

"No, ma'am."

"Has something new developed in my case?"

"Not exactly. We got hold of the guard who had the day shift yesterday. He swears no strangers came into the lobby while he was here. Of course, he left his post several times, but never for more than a few minutes, he says, and the foyer door was locked."

"But you said somebody who knows locks could get in in less than a minute," Darcy reminded him.

"That's true. A good security system cuts down on crime, but no system is one hundred percent effective. Have you thought any more about getting an alarm system?"

"I'm going to check into it tomorrow."

"I talked to your ex-husband this morning," the officer went on. "He claims to have been with a lady friend yesterday from before noon until about eight o'clock last night. Says she'll corroborate his story. Gave me her name and number. I'll follow up on it, but I have to tell you I believe him, Miss Gilbert."

"Bill can be very convincing," Darcy said. "I used to believe his lies, too."

"You don't seem to have any doubt that it's Bainbridge who's doing this."

"No, I haven't."

"I'll keep on it." He rose to leave. "Call me immediately if you get any more notes or phone calls," he said as he went to the door.

"He hasn't phoned since I had my number changed. I'm being very cautious about who I give the number to."

"Good, but if he does call, we can put a tap on your phone and try to trace future calls."

After the officer left, Darcy pulled on boots, a warm coat and gloves and went to the supermarket to buy the ingredients for her dinner with Zach that evening. A light dusting of dry snow had fallen during the night. Yards glistened with whiteness, but the streets were already clear.

She purchased crabmeat and shrimp for seafood crepes, which she would serve topped with a shrimp and green noodle sauce. With the crepes, they'd have a spinach salad, julienne carrots and hot rolls. For dessert, she'd make chocolate mousse with a brandied raspberry sauce. She even remembered to buy candles for the table.

She spent the afternoon preparing the meal. When she got to Zach's, she'd only have to pop the main course into the oven.

As she dressed for the evening, she was aware of a nervy expectancy. Her skin was unusually sensitive to the brush of the silk fabric as she buttoned a lace-trimmed cream blouse and pulled a deep blue swirling skirt over her head. She took extra care with her makeup and brushed her hair until it lay in loose, shining waves on her shoulders, exactly as she wanted it to.

She turned in front of the full-length mirror in her bedroom, at last satisfied with her appearance. She looked ready for a romantic evening, and felt like it, too. She'd never been particularly intrigued by romance until just lately, when she'd caught herself drawn to romantic gestures, like the candles she'd bought for the dinner table.

Apparently romantic gestures were in the air, for when she arrived at Zach's he met her with a kiss and a dozen long-stemmed red roses.

"Oh, Zach, they're perfectly lovely," she exclaimed as she buried her face among the velvet buds. "We must put them on the dinner table. Do you have a vase?"

He found a crystal vase in the top of his cabinet and presented it to her. "What else can I do for you, beautiful lady?"

She kissed his cheek. "Get the food out of my car," she told him, "while I take off my coat and set the oven."

Zach had arranged a card table with a white linen cloth and napkins in the den. They ate by candlelight.

She told him about the visit from Officer Link that morning.

"Maybe Bill is telling the truth, about being with a woman when that note was slipped under your door," Zach observed. "It'd be pretty stupid to give the police the woman's name if he wasn't sure she'd back him up."

"He could have coached her on what to say."

"Then she'd be pretty stupid to go along with him and lie to the police."

"He could talk her into it. You don't know how he twists things. He's probably convinced her I'm meanness personified and deserve to be scared witless."

He gazed at her for a moment. "Honey, I think you have to at least consider the possibility that Bill isn't doing these things."

"I've tried to. Honestly I have. There just isn't anyone else."

"It could be somebody you don't even know, someone who became obsessed with you after seeing you on television."

She shook her head. "No, the first contact was made on the hot line, where he knew me as Jo. I don't know how he connected me with Jo, but—"

"Maybe your voice gave you away. Chances are he's seen you on television many times. When he talked to you on the hot line, he could have recognized your voice."

But how did he know to ask for Jo in the first place? Impatiently, Darcy shook the question aside. She didn't want the caller to intrude on the evening. She just wanted to relax and enjoy being with Zach.

What had she done with her weekends before she knew Zach? Nothing much, as she recalled, but she didn't remember feeling lonely. She had not thought she was missing anything by keeping to herself. Zach had shown her she was wrong on that score, at least.

Zach's earnest tone interrupted her wandering thoughts. "Promise me you'll be careful, especially when you're away from the station and your apartment."

"I am being careful," she assured him. "Tomorrow I'm going to order an alarm system for the apartment."

"Good. I have to be out of town next weekend—a trauma medicine conference in Boston. I wish it hadn't come up just now, but I don't think I can get out of it."

Darcy's disappointment was sharp. A whole weekend without seeing Zach would be long and depressing. She knew it was silly to feel that way. She and Zach still had full, separate lives apart from each other. That was the way she wanted it, wasn't it?

"Zach, don't even consider changing your plans. I don't want you to worry about me."

"Tell the wind not to blow, Darcy."

Darcy shook her head in mock exasperation. She considered the interesting possibilities of the analogy. Then she thought about being separated from Zach for two weeks. When Zach was on the day shift, as he was now, their schedules made seeing each other during the week difficult.

Tonight was special, then. She wanted to fill it with enough memories to warm her for two weeks. She wanted to appreciate every moment.

Thereafter, she continued to eat but tasted little of the meal. She was too full of thoughts of Zach. He kept her wineglass filled with something smooth and mellow, but it might have been water for all it mattered. Vaguely she was aware of the way her pale skin and silk blouse captured the candlelight; she had never felt more a woman or more grateful for it. Zach's eyes caressed her constantly, telling her that she was desirable. His eyes warmed her, and she felt as though she was being wooed for the very first time.

He made her smile softly with a word or the touch of his hand on hers. With a look he made her face glow, her skin flush with pleasure. How could she ever have thought candlelight and flowers frivolous sentimental gestures? When you were with the right man, they became grandly romantic. Had she been less naive in matters of the heart or more honest with herself, she would have realized that she was falling in love.

They lingered over dessert even though neither of them could have said what they were eating. The candles burned low, the wax dripping in teardrops over the crystal holders. The last of the wine warmed in their glasses. Darcy sat spellbound by Zach's expressive eyes.

He could not get his fill of watching her in the flickering light. He loved the sound of her quiet voice flowing over him. His fingers caressed the back of her hand. He loved the satiny softness of her skin. He felt as though they had all the time in the world, and for the moment he wanted only to be with her.

The fire of passion would be there when they chose to release it. It was never very far away when he was with her. He would take her to his bed in the dark and imagine how it would be to have her there every night for the rest of his life.

When they had finished the mousse, he took both her hands in his, turning them palms up to receive his lips. "I'll take care of the dishes. You relax."

His hot breath in her palm sent delight shivering up her arm. "Let me help you." Given a choice, she would have had him forget the dishes altogether.

"No, you made the meal. I'll clean up." Lifting his head, he closed her fingers over the warmth from his mouth that lingered in the palm. "Make yourself at home and wait for me, love."

Darcy rose, and in a daze wandered through the house. It was the second time he'd called her "love." More than any other, the endearment set her heart beating so rapidly it made her feel weak. Faint with pleasure and the anticipation of more pleasure, she reflected, as she ran her hand over the face of the fireplace. The stones were rough and warm. She fingered a carved duck on the mantel. The polished wood felt sleek and cool to her fingers.

All her senses were incredibly alert tonight. It was a night made for sensation, for feeling, she thought, as she left the room to move dreamily down the hall. A night made for romance and love.

She entered Zach's bedroom, saw the big bed looming in the shadows. This was the room where they'd first made love. Her footsteps were muffled by the thick carpet as she went to the window. She touched the cool pane. Beyond the glass a few stars pricked the dark sky. The moon was a golden crescent. It was so quiet she could hear tree limbs crackle in the cold air.

She imagined herself and Zach shut away from the world. Suppose there were no television station, no hospital, no medical conference in Boston, no threats whispered into a telephone, no dark sedans following her, no terrifying notes slipped under her door.

Suppose there were only she and Zach, alone together in some remote place where no one could find them.

She wandered into the adjoining bathroom, switched on the light and gazed into the reflection of her own dark eyes in the mirror. She looked a bit drunk, stunned by emotion. She smiled at the thought and turned away to bury her face in Zach's robe hanging from a hook on the door. With a sigh, she inhaled his scent and pressed her cheek against the brown terry cloth.

Leaving the bathroom, she pulled the door nearly closed behind her. Turning, she looked around the bedroom. The light filtering around the crack in the door was pale and insubstantial. Shadows shifted mysteriously in corners. Romantic, she thought. Everything seemed romantic tonight. Strange how the environment changed, depending on your mood.

Red numerals glowed at her from the digital clock radio on the bedside table. She drifted to the table and turned on the radio, running the dial until she found a station playing quiet mood music. She turned the volume low, and kicking off her shoes, curled on her side on the bed. She began to hum along with the mellow strains of a love song.

Zach heard faint music as he came down the hall. He halted in the bedroom doorway, letting his eyes adjust to the semidarkness. She was lying on his bed, her face toward the door, her eyes closed. Her hair was a dark cloud around her pale face. She was so lovely it made his throat ache.

It was an enchanted moment, and he hesitated in the doorway, reluctant to break the spell. He wanted to hold the moment forever. He would always remember her like this, he thought, so beautiful, with the soft dreamy strains of a love song floating around her.

He moved toward the bed. "Darcy," he whispered. She opened her eyes and looked at him. She stretched lazily and smiled.

She reached out a hand. "I've been waiting for you. What took you so long?"

"It's only been a few minutes." Zach realized he was still whispering, careful not to shatter the gentle spell that filled the shadowy room. He took her hand and sat on the bed beside her.

"It seemed much longer," she murmured.

He leaned over her, only their hands touching still, and let his gaze roam her lovely face. She smiled with that sweet warmth in her eyes that turned his insides to jelly.

"I'll always remember you like this," he whispered. "So beautiful it frightens me. I can't believe you're real and that you're here with me."

She brought his hand to her cheek. "Oh, I'm real, and I'm exactly where I want to be," she murmured.

"What were you thinking when I came in?"

"I was daydreaming—pretending we'd run away where no one can find us. Imagining we could stay as long as we like."

The wistful tone of her voice moved him. Tenderness washed through him. He stroked her cheek. Her skin was soft and warm to his touch. "I feel as though I've waited for this moment all my life."

With her fingertips, she traced one hard cheekbone wonderingly. "Perhaps I have, too. Odd . . . I'll have to think about what that means."

Her eyes were dark and brilliant in the dim light, like black diamonds. Zach cupped her face in his hand. "Do you ever think about past lives?"

"No."

"I never did until I met you. Now I wonder if we were lovers in a former life. Perhaps that's why it feels so right when we're together. As though I've come home." He kissed her forehead, then her cheeks, taking his time.

Her mouth trembled for the taste of him. "Yes..."
Her voice wavered. "It is like that. Sometimes . . . oh,
sometimes I wish we really could run away . . ."

"We have." At last he kissed her mouth. "Right
now, tonight, we're on a distant star, spinning through
space. There's nobody here but us." He brushed his
lips over her eyelids.

"What a lovely dream."

"It's no dream. We'll make it real."

"Yes. We'll create our own world, make it exactly
as we want it to be," she whispered. "How shall we
start?"

"With love," he murmured, lying down beside her.
"Like this."

A long time later, Darcy put on Zach's robe. It
touched the floor, and she had to roll the sleeves up
several times to see her hands. But she loved the feel
of it against her naked skin. Zach built a fire in the
fireplace, and she curled into his lap in a big armchair
in front of it.

"Stay with me all night," he whispered against her
hair.

It would be so easy to say yes. She had never wanted
anything more. She hated the thought of getting
dressed again and driving through the cold night to her
apartment alone. So she thought about it for several
moments.

At last, she said regretfully, "I need a change of
clothes for tomorrow, and I like to be at the station
earlier on Mondays so I can get a handle on the week."

"Then will you think about going to Boston with me next weekend?"

"Let's concentrate on now, Zach. I can stay another hour or two."

Zach let it go. He didn't want to spoil their time together by regretting that it couldn't be more.

Chapter 13

Darcy and Zach met for lunch the next Thursday in a restaurant near the hospital. Zach had only a forty-five minute break from his shift at the trauma center. The restaurant was crowded and noisy, which made talking difficult. Darcy had hoped for quiet and intimate conversation, and the hurried meeting was less than satisfying.

"I'm flying to Boston tomorrow evening," Zach told her as they walked to her car. "I'll call you Saturday or Saturday night."

They kissed hungrily. "Damn," Zach muttered, "I wish you were coming with me."

"I couldn't find anyone to install the alarm system until Saturday. I have to be there."

He held her for another moment. It was probably a good idea for them to be separated for a few days, he told himself. Ever since he met Darcy, he'd felt as though he was being carried along by a tidal wave. So many things seemed speeded up, the time he spent with Darcy, the intensity of his feelings. By contrast, when he was separated from her the hours seemed endless. He thought about her, ached for her, all the time. A little distance seemed called for.

"Will you be working days again next week?"

"Yes, unfortunately." Before meeting Darcy, he, like most of the other doctors, had preferred the day shift. Now, because of her schedule, working days meant he couldn't see as much of Darcy as he'd like. It wasn't fair to expect her to see him after eleven at night when she left work, tired and often stressed. Television news, he was learning, could be as hectic as trauma center medicine, especially when stories were fast-breaking. And hasty lunches like today's were more frustrating than satisfying.

"Maybe I'll see if Jill's free for shopping or a movie this weekend. I haven't seen much of her away from work since she started dating Charles."

He kissed her one last time and set her away from him. "I have to go."

"I'll drop you off at the hospital."

"It's faster to cut through the park. Goodbye, love." The endearment came automatically now, but Darcy savored it.

He left her, running across the restaurant parking lot and along one of the winding paths that criss-crossed the park.

Having nothing better to do, Darcy went directly to the station from the restaurant. Jill hurried toward her, left hand extended, as Darcy was hanging up her coat. A diamond solitaire sparkled on Jill's ring finger. It was almost as bright as the sparkle in Jill's eyes.

"Charles finally popped the question."

"Congratulations!" Darcy hugged her. "I'm not exactly surprised. You two have been as close as Siamese twins the past three months. Just be happy, you hear?"

"I'm practically delirious. I feel so fortunate."

"Charles is the lucky one. Don't you forget it. Have you set the date?"

"New Year's Day. We're having a small ceremony. Just family and close friends. But still, there's a lot to do in such a short time." The words bubbled out of Jill like frothy champagne. "Charles' sister is going to help me pick out my wedding dress Saturday, and then we're meeting Charles and his parents for dinner. Oh, I'm so excited I almost forgot—will you be my maid of honor?"

"I'll be delighted."

It sounded as though Jill would be hip-deep in wedding preparations all weekend. Darcy abandoned her hope to spend time with her friend while Zach was out of town. She would have to rely on her own resources to fill up the time.

Saturday morning, two men arrived at the apartment to install the new alarm system. All the windows were wired, and motion detectors were installed at both doors. A small red light shone outside and inside the two doors when the system was turned on. Darcy had opted not to have the system connected to the police station, since there would be a security guard on duty any time the alarm sounded.

"You turn it off with this key," one of the men told Darcy as he was returning tools to his tool chest. "Here." He stepped into the hall and showed her the two keyholes newly installed in the door facing. "The bottom one's for the motion detectors. The top one's for the rest of the system. There are two more beside the back door. Inside, you turn off the system with the two switches beside each door. Don't forget to keep the motion detectors turned off while you're here. When this thing goes off, you'll be able to hear it for blocks. Any questions?"

"No. It seems simple enough." Another key to turn before she could enter the apartment, but that inconvenience was a small price to pay for the added security.

"Here're a couple extra keys. You should leave one at the security station in the lobby, in case the alarm goes off when you're away."

After the installers left, Darcy took one of the keys to the guard on duty. Back in her apartment, she added a key to her key ring and placed the other in the desk, conveniently close to the front door.

She made lunch and drove to the nearest bookstore, where she bought two best-selling novels recently reprinted in paperback. Though she hadn't done much recreational reading lately, she had always been able to lose herself in a good book.

The first novel proved to be less than engrossing, so she abandoned it for the second. When she found her attention wandering from the second book, she realized the problem wasn't with the novels. It was with her. She was missing Zach. She was sorry she hadn't made other arrangements for having the alarm system installed and gone with him to Boston.

She laid her book aside and wandered through the apartment, checking the alarm system. The motion detectors were disengaged, since she might inadvertently set them off while moving around the apartment, but the red lights were on, indicating that the rest of the system was operational. All was as it should be.

She made herself a cup of hot lemon tea and sat at the kitchen table, gazing out at the courtyard. A gust of wind rattled the branches of the trees and drove the fallen leaves before it across the grass.

What was Zach doing right now? And who was he doing it with? There were a lot of female doctors these days.

The thought made her feel foolish. Was she actually jealous? For heaven's sake, jealousy was such a petty emotion. Besides, she trusted Zach implicitly. It wasn't that she thought he'd seek out another woman in Boston. But it was frustrating to think that other women could be near him—see him, talk to him—while she was here, alone.

This was the first time they'd been separated since they'd started spending so much time together. With Zach in Boston, it felt as though an important part of her life was missing.

The discovery made her a bit uncomfortable, and she tried to understand why. What it boiled down to, it seemed, was that she no longer felt like a whole person alone. She needed Zach. She had never meant for that to happen. She hadn't really believed it could.

Was it such a terrible thing to need someone?

From one point of view, it was scary. She was vulnerable now. Zach could hurt her. On the other hand, it could mean she'd made a step forward, that she'd finally rid herself of the emotional hang-ups left by her marriage. It could mean she'd recovered fully, that the unhappy memories of her time with Bill no longer had any influence in her life.

She preferred to take the positive point of view, she decided.

She jumped when the telephone rang at seven Saturday evening and ran to snatch it up. "Zach?"

"Were you expecting someone else?"

With a little sigh of pleasure, she sank into a chair, "I don't think I'll answer that. A woman should maintain an air of mystery. Otherwise, men will take her for granted."

"I can't imagine any man ever taking you for granted," he said huskily.

His voice was almost a caress. It sent a little shiver up her spine. "What did you do today?"

"Listened to speakers. Deadly boring, some of them."

"I'm sorry if you aren't enjoying the conference."

"I don't enjoy being away from you."

"I don't enjoy it much, either."

"Good," he said with satisfaction. "How are things there otherwise?"

"Fine. The alarm system's in. I feel very safe." She ran her finger around the telephone mouthpiece, wishing it were Zach's mouth. "I think I'll work on the hot line tomorrow, just to have something to do."

"Be careful," he said automatically. "Don't stay out after dark."

"Yes, master," she said, smiling.

He laughed then. "Master, my eye. I'm your slave, Darcy Gilbert."

"Oh, that's nice," she murmured. "I've never had a slave before. I think I can get into it."

"Gad, you've got a streak of power hunger in you," he said with a chuckle. "Remember, though, no chains or whips."

"I don't think I'll need them."

"Hmm, no." He grew serious. "God, I miss you."

"When will I see you?"

"My return flight's due in at six-forty Monday morning. I'll go directly to the hospital from the airport. I tried to trade shifts with somebody Monday, but no dice. I did manage to get Tuesday off. We could have a long lunch for a change. Some place quiet and intimate."

"My apartment is quiet and intimate."

"Are you, by chance, laying plans to seduce me?"

Her heartbeat quickened at the lazily seductive tone of his voice. "Come off it, Dr. Shaffer. I don't have to *plan*."

He heaved an elaborate sigh. "I'm easy, I admit it. Can't seem to help myself."

Her laugh was a bit shaky. "As a slave, you have no choice in the matter," she reminded him.

"As my master, you are now responsible for my creature comforts."

"Bull," she said airily. "I decide what I'm responsible for. That's what a master does. Don't you know anything about this master-slave business, Dr. Shaffer?"

"Apparently not. Well . . . I'm supposed to meet a couple of people for dinner."

"Female people?"

"One is."

"What's she look like?"

"Green eyes, flaming red hair." She could detect a grin in his voice.

"I'd hate her," Darcy confessed.

"On the contrary. Dr. Carson is a likable lady. Always joking. Even jokes about her size—she weighs roughly three hundred pounds."

"Oh. You run along and have a good time, then," Darcy purred. "About Tuesday. Instead of lunch, why don't we have brunch—then you can come at ten without appearing too eager. Shall we?"

"Let's. If I can break free, I'll call you Monday before you leave for work."

"All right. Good night, Zach."

"Sweet dreams," he murmured before he hung up.

Sunday, Darcy worked on the hot line from ten to four in the afternoon, two hours longer than her regular Thursday-night shift. But volunteers often worked overtime on weekends, when it was difficult to find enough people to answer the phones.

For most of the day, Darcy and the young college student, Phil, handled incoming calls alone, keeping people on hold for as long as ten minutes. During a brief lull about noon, Darcy called Betina, who agreed to come down at two and stay four or five hours. Two other volunteers were scheduled to come in at five.

Betina arrived with three cups of coffee in Styrofoam cups and a batch of brownies still warm from the oven.

"Caffeine!" Phil exclaimed, grabbing one of the cups. They'd been too busy the past two hours to make coffee. "And sugar!" He lifted a brownie from the plate Betina sat on the table. "Reminds me of my breakfast. The fuel that keeps the old machine going."

"You have atrocious eating habits," Betina told him, an oft-repeated refrain. "They'll catch up with you one of these days."

"Like those coffin nails you smoke?"

"Don't change the subject, Phil. You'll wish you'd listened to me when your hair and teeth start to fall out."

Phil merely grinned, licked his fingers and reached for another brownie with one hand as he answered his phone with the other.

Darcy blew on her coffee before taking a drink. "Mmm, I needed that. Thanks, Betina." The phone rang and she turned to the table. "Domestic Violence Hot Line. This is Jo."

"You can't hide from me with that fake name, Darcy." The voice was gravelly, muffled. His breathing sounded labored, but perhaps that was because he had his mouth pressed to the receiver in order to be heard through whatever filter he was using to disguise his voice.

Darcy gripped the receiver hard. How had he known she would be on the hot line today? She hadn't known it herself until yesterday. He must have followed her there. That's the only way he could have known. But she hadn't been aware of being followed.

"No more than you can hide your identity by disguising your voice," she retorted. "I know who you are. So do the police."

He was silent for a long moment. She could hear him breathing into the phone. "You're no good at bluffing, either. You know nothing. Face it, I'm too clever for you."

"You're not clever. You're sick. You need help."

"Don't say that, you stupid bitch!" The words crackled with fury. "What I need is for people to stop messing with my life! I won't let 'em get away with it. I won't let *you*, Darcy."

She decided to try reason. "That's your paranoia talking. Nobody's messing with your life. You're the problem, nobody else."

He laughed, kept on laughing as though he couldn't stop. A high cackle, almost a keening. He sounded like a maniac who needed to be chained up. Then he stopped abruptly, panting to catch his breath. "I know you're scared, Darcy. You thought you could get rid of me by changing your phone number. But I got into your building, didn't I?"

"The police have that note."

"That won't stop me! I can get in again, whenever I want. All your locks and your uniformed guards can't keep me out."

Cold fear trembled through Darcy. It was followed by hot anger. What right did he have to terrorize her? Why did she have to be the one to give him his cheap thrills? "Don't try it," she blurted. "You got lucky the first time, but I have something better than locks and uniformed guards now."

He breathed into the phone. Then, "You won't shoot me, Darcy. You don't have the guts to pull the trigger."

He thought she had a gun. Well, so much the better. "Don't count on it!" She hung up.

"The nut case again?" Betina asked.

At the sound of the other woman's voice, Darcy started. For a few moments there had been no one but her and that raspy voice on the telephone.

"I can tell by the look on your face that it was. I didn't know he was still calling you."

"It's the first time he's called in a while."

"You'd better report it to the police."

"I intend to." Darcy reached for the phone. She didn't think reporting this conversation would provide the police with any new clues to the caller's identity, but she'd promised Officer Link.

When she got home, the security guard on duty assured her the building had been quiet all day. Few people had come in, and those who had were either residents or frequent visitors known to the guard.

Once she was inside her apartment with the alarm system activated, Darcy found herself compulsively checking locks. She forced herself to stop. It was obvious nobody had been in the apartment since she'd left.

She was letting the anonymous caller accomplish exactly what he'd set out to do. Her nerves were shot. She had to get her mind on something else.

After soaking in a bubble bath for twenty minutes, she donned her warmest robe, a flowing red velour trimmed with white lace. Though she'd had no lunch, Betina's brownies had dampened her appetite. She prepared a light snack of buttered toast and hot chocolate.

Loading the food on a tray, she carried it to the living-room couch and picked up one of the novels she'd started yesterday. She'd finish it this evening, she vowed. That should fill up the hours until it was time to go to bed.

She put the book down shortly before eleven and slept through the night undisturbed.

Zach phoned from the hospital during his lunch break Monday. The mere sound of his voice was comforting to Darcy, and she decided not to tell him about Sunday's phone call until they were together Tuesday.

"Mom wants to know if you can spend Thanksgiving with us in Rogers," Zach told her.

Thanksgiving was just ten days away, Darcy realized. She'd forgotten about it with everything else that had been going on. But then she hadn't really looked forward to holidays the past few years. "Did you tell her to invite me?"

"I mentioned that we'd been seeing quite a lot of each other." He hesitated. "You don't have other plans for Thanksgiving, do you?"

"No."

When she didn't go on, he said, "You don't have to give me an answer now. Let me know in a few days."

"I will. Zach, you sound exhausted."

"I don't sleep well in hotels," he admitted. "I'll crash as soon as I get off work, and dream of you."

She smiled. "What will we do, in your dream?"

"I'll tell you tomorrow, in great detail. See you at ten."

Slowly, Darcy opened her eyes. The room was black. She couldn't have been asleep long. It had been a particularly hectic Monday at the station. She'd barely had enough energy left to undress before falling into bed at eleven-thirty.

Something had awakened her. Maybe an ambulance siren or a dog barking.

She closed her eyes. She didn't want to move, didn't want to do anything that would further disturb her warm drowsiness. She'd end up checking all the locks again.

Stop thinking, she ordered herself. Go back to sleep.

She dropped off again. She was floating in a warm sea, the waves lapping around her, lulling her with a feeling of sated slothfulness.

Something was pulling her from the soothing water. She tried to fight it. Then, abruptly, she jerked awake again.

She sat up, feeling for the lamp beside the bed. She switched it on and reached for the robe at the foot of the bed. Something had wakened her. Perhaps it had been something in her dream. But she wouldn't be able to sleep until she'd checked the apartment.

Pushing her feet into scuffs, she moved cautiously through the rooms, turning on lights as she went. By the time she reached the living room, the apartment was blazing with light and she'd found nothing amiss.

It was then that she noticed the door to the coat closet was slightly ajar. She always kept it closed. She tried to shake off the creeping dread that slithered over her skin. What did the open door mean?

She'd failed to close the closet door for once, that was all, she assured herself. But she wasn't quite convinced. She frowned, knowing she would never be able to go back to bed without checking the closet.

She took a step toward the closet and felt a waft of cold air on her back. She whirled around. There was a barely perceptible billow in the closed drapery. She knew she hadn't left the window open.

She was nearly certain, anyway. Maybe she'd opened it and forgotten. She'd been so on edge the past couple of days, almost anything was possible.

She swallowed the dryness in her mouth, walked resolutely to the window and swept the drapery back. It was closed, but one of the small panes was broken. Darcy stared at the jagged hole, big enough to admit a human hand.

The alarm system had failed!

Gripped by the most acute terror she'd ever known, Darcy whirled and rushed to the phone on the desk. The number of the security station in the lobby was taped on the back of the receiver. Repeating the number to herself, she snatched up the receiver. There was no dial tone. She jabbed the disconnect button furiously, but still no tone. The line was dead. She lifted the receiver higher and saw the blunt end of the telephone line dangling uselessly down the side of the desk. It had been cut.

He was in the apartment!

She ran for the door. She was halfway across the room when a stranger stepped out of the coat closet. She froze in her tracks.

The glitter in his eyes could have kindled firewood. Was it fury? Madness? "Hello, Darcy. Didn't I tell you I could get in whenever I wanted to?"

He was short and stocky with a thick neck and long arms. Though he wore a loose-fitting jacket, she could tell they were powerful arms. She choked back an impulse to scream for help. Screaming might send him over the edge. Screaming was a last resort.

She tried to calculate which she had a better chance of reaching before he caught her—the door opening on the hallway or the bedroom.

"You ruined my life, Darcy, and now you're gonna pay. Did you really think an alarm system would protect you? It took me about two minutes to disconnect it."

"Who are you?" Her voice shook so badly the words were barely understandable.

"You made Claire leave me. I haven't seen my kids in six weeks. I can't even find them."

"You're Claire's husband?" Darcy tried to gauge the distance to the front door. She might reach it before he could stop her, but could she release the chain and dead bolt in time? Her hands were shaking so badly she wasn't even sure she could get a grip on the bolt. She clenched her hands into fists to stop the shaking.

Ralph Champlin watched her alertly. He seemed poised, waiting. Waiting for what? For Darcy to make a break?

Darcy tried to speak with a semblance of calmness and reason. "It was Claire's decision to leave."

"I found the hot line number with Jo written beside it after she left. She'd written another number below that. I called the hot line and asked for Jo. As soon as I heard your voice, I knew I'd heard it before."

Apparently he wanted to spell it out for her so she would see how clever he'd been.

"It wasn't till I saw you on TV later that I put it together. So I called the other number, and you answered. It was the number at this apartment—till you changed it."

Darcy listened with only half her mind. The other half was thinking frantically that she had to do something before he stopped talking. The bedroom seemed her best chance. The Mace canister was on the bedside table. It could buy her enough time to get out of the apartment.

"You picked the lock in the lobby door when you found out I had a new number."

"Easy as pie." He snorted. "I just waited till the guard was outside—a couple of twists and I was in. The alarm system took a little longer, but not much. I'll find Claire and my kids, too—after I take care of you."

Darcy saw his hands flexing and blurted, "She didn't want to leave you. You gave her no choice. If you'll get help, she might come back to you."

His face reddened. "Help! You're the one who needs help!"

It was hopeless to try to dispel his hostility with reason. He knew only one way to relieve it. Violence.

Darcy made a dash for the bedroom. She heard his furious shout of surprise as she stumbled through the doorway and crashed the door shut behind her. Somehow she succeeded in making her shaking fingers turn the lock. But it wouldn't hold long if he decided to break in.

"Help!" Her scream shattered the night stillness. "Somebody help me!"

She ran around the bed and snatched at the Mace canister. The canister slipped through her fingers, fell to the floor and rolled under the bed.

He banged on the bedroom door with his fist. Then he stepped back and lunged at it. The door shook. Darcy dropped to her knees and half crawled under the bed, searching for the Mace canister.

Another thud and the sound of wood splintering again. She couldn't reach the canister. She backed from beneath the bed. She couldn't risk going around the bed to get it. Time had run out. She raced for the bathroom as she heard the door crack and Champlin crashed through.

She locked the bathroom door and began to yell for help again. Where was the security guard? Why couldn't someone hear her? She threw open the medicine cabinet in search of something, anything, she could use as a weapon.

Cursing violently, Champlin lunged at the bathroom door.

Darcy's hand closed around the can of hair spray. A pitiful weapon, but it was all she had. That and surprise. She didn't give herself time to think. She yelled, "Champlin, I have a gun! Don't make me use it!"

In a single swift movement, she unlocked the door and threw it open. The door hit his face and he staggered back. She had the hair spray ready. The instant she had a clear shot at his shocked face, she aimed at his eyes. He shrieked, clutched his face and stumbled against the bed. Darcy darted around him and out of the room.

As she reached the front door, she heard the guard's voice. "Miss Gilbert? Miss Gilbert, are you all right?" She released the chain, turned the dead bolt and threw open the door.

The guard held a revolver. Behind him, a neighbor in her robe was edging warily out of her apartment.

"He broke in," Darcy gasped. "He's in my bedroom." The guard slipped past her and Darcy fell into her neighbor's arms.

It was over in fifteen minutes. Ralph Champlin was subdued as the police led him out of the building. Hearing Darcy's screams, the security guard had called the station before he came to the apartment. The sight of his gun had defused Champlin's anger instantly and kept him in hand until the police arrived.

The neighbor clucked over Darcy, patting her back and saying, "Poor little thing. Everything's all right now." They were in the neighbor's living room, the door open to the hall, so they saw the police lead Champlin away.

The security guard stopped at the open door. "Did he hurt you, Miss Gilbert?"

"No, he just scared me to death."

"No wonder," clucked the neighbor, "poor little thing."

"I didn't hear the alarm, Miss Gilbert," the guard said.

"He disconnected it. He came in from the courtyard."

"I never heard a thing till you started screaming."

"It wasn't your fault," Darcy said.

The guard's worried frown eased somewhat. "I'll nail something over that broken window till you can get the pane replaced. Is there anything I can get you?" he asked. "Anything I can do for you?"

"There is one thing," Darcy said. "Would you please call Dr. Shaffer. Ask him to come over. Tell him—tell him I need him."

Chapter 14

When Zach arrived twenty minutes later, the broken window pane had been covered with a piece of plywood and Darcy had returned to her apartment.

She'd stopped shaking. She thought she had herself well under control. But the sight of Zach undid her. He wore hastily donned warm-ups. His hair was still rumpled from sleep, and his brow was deeply creased with worry.

She hadn't known she was going to cry. The tears started to fall as she was folded in his embrace.

"It's all right, sweetheart." He led her to the couch and pulled her down across his lap, cradling her in his arms. He was saying something quiet and comforting. It didn't matter what the words were. It was their sound that soothed her. She closed her eyes and clung to him.

Zach felt her body relax against him. He'd died a thousand deaths on that reckless drive to her apartment. The security guard had said she wasn't hurt, but he couldn't believe it until he saw her with his own eyes.

"Shh. It's all right, love. It's all right now."

Darcy nodded and swallowed a sob. She wiped her eyes on the sleeve of her robe.

He stroked her hair. "The guard said it was some guy named Champlin. Who is he?"

She sat up a little straighter. Her composure was returning. "Claire Champlin's husband. She's the woman I brought to the emergency room with a broken arm."

"My God—I didn't make the connection."

"Claire left behind the paper where she'd written the hot line number and my home phone number when she left her husband and went to the shelter with her children. They're still there. She's planning a future without Ralph."

"Good," he said grimly.

"He—he found the phone numbers and started calling the hot line. He recognized my voice from TV. Remember, you said it could have happened that way? Then he called here, and after I had the number changed, he got in through the foyer and left that note. Tonight he broke a window."

She spoke rapidly, her words tumbling out as though it brought her some relief to say them. "It's over now, Darcy."

"He blames me for the loss of his family."

"That's insane."

She nodded. "I was so sure it was Bill..." Seized by sudden restlessness, she disengaged herself and rose. "I'll have to apologize to him. As for Champlin, maybe he'll get psychiatric help now."

He felt her withdrawal. Why wouldn't she look at him suddenly? "What's wrong, Darcy?"

It all seemed to hit her at once, and she had found she couldn't meet his gaze squarely. Tonight while she fought paralyzing fear and struggled for her life, thinking of Zach had given her the necessary courage. When it was over, all she could think of was Zach. She wanted to be with him. She wanted his arms around her. Now that he was there, it seemed to take more courage to face the man she loved than it had taken to face a violently deranged man.

The man she loved. The words filled her mind. She'd learned to trust Zach over the past several weeks, but before tonight, she'd not been able to take that final step of acknowledging to herself that she was in love with him. Now she'd done it, and she couldn't go back. But being in love didn't automatically lead to happily ever after. There was the question of Zach's feelings. Were they as deep as her own? There was also the problem of how to mesh love and the independence she'd come to prize.

"I'm sorry your sleep was disturbed," she said. "It was all over when I asked the guard to call you. I don't know what came over me. Silly of me to roust you out of bed. I—I wasn't thinking too clearly."

He got to his feet. "The guard said you needed me. Did you tell him to say that?"

"I suppose I must have."

He moved toward her, stopping within touching distance. But he didn't touch her. "I'll always come when you need me, Darcy."

She stared at him. "You will?"

"Count on it."

"I'm scared, Zach."

"That's understandable, but you're safe now."

She shook her head. "No, I don't mean that. Tonight, I needed you desperately. I needed to feel your arms around me and to have you tell me everything was all right. It was a—a compulsion. That's what scares me."

His hands clenched at his sides. "You think it's any different for me? Driving here tonight, I was frantic, wondering if you were really unhurt. The guard assured me you were, but I had to see for myself. I had to touch you and hear you say that maniac didn't harm you. All the assurances in the world from a third party wouldn't have sufficed. That kind of need is new to me."

"There's something that scares me even more. It's thinking of a life without you."

"You don't have to."

When he tried to take her in his arms, she pulled away. To force back the tears, she pressed her fingers to her eyes. "I never meant to be dependent on you, Zach. It makes me feel I've lost control of my life. I'm not comfortable with the feeling."

He drew her to him and this time she didn't pull away. Curling his hand beneath her chin, he tilted her face up to his. "I love you, Darcy. Tell me you love me, too. Say the words."

Tears filled her eyes. "Is it that obvious? I've tried to fight it, you know. I never meant to fall in love, ever again."

"I need to hear the words."

She drew in a jagged breath. "I love you."

A tear rolled down her cheek and he kissed it away. "Don't cry," he pleaded. "We love each other. That's no cause for grieving."

She held him close until the tightness in her chest eased. "I'm not very good at love," she whispered. "It makes me feel defenseless."

"Sweetheart, love is two people sharing their lives. It's not a struggle for control."

She lifted her face, and he touched it gently with his fingertips. She blinked back more tears. "It's hard for me to share my life, Zach. Can you be patient with me while I learn?"

With a muttered oath, he clasped her face in his big hands and kissed her passionately. "Marry me, Darcy. We can work it out if we're together."

She tilted her head back and looked at him, her eyes wide. "Oh, Zach, I'm not even used to the idea of being in love yet, and you're talking about marriage."

"Getting married is what people do when they love each other."

"Maybe most people do. But—couldn't we take it a step at a time? To start with, I'll go home with you for Thanksgiving."

He brushed his lips over her temple. "Wearing my engagement ring?"

Things were moving so quickly Darcy's head swam. Yet if she couldn't even accept a symbol of their love, had she really put the past behind her? And how deeply did she trust Zach? Enough to make a commitment?

"An engagement is a serious step. I'm going to need some time—" She broke off when she saw the tension in his face. "For one thing, our working schedules will make things difficult."

A hint of a smile softened the tightness around his mouth. "Schedules can be worked around. I won't let you put me off, Darcy. I want an answer now. Yes or no?"

Her answering smile formed slowly. "We could have a long engagement, I suppose."

"Is that a yes?"

She nodded gravely. "I think it is."

He bent down until his lips hovered an inch from hers. "Think?" The question was teasing, but there was an undertone of uncertainty in it.

Darcy searched his eyes, and he hers. Each found what he was looking for—trust, love, commitment. "It's definitely a yes."

His lips curved. "That wasn't so hard, was it?"

"No," she whispered and wound her arms around his neck.

His gaze dropped to her mouth, lingered, then rose. "I'm going to change your mind about that long engagement, you know."

She cocked a brow. "How?"

Without a word, he lifted her, carried her to the bedroom and dropped her unceremoniously on the bed. Bending over her, he opened her robe. "I have my ways."

"Well, perhaps six months—"

His mouth silenced her in a long, lingering kiss as his body settled unerringly over hers. "That's not just long, it's an eternity. One month."

"Three." She sighed. "I could probably get used to the idea of marriage in three months."

"Two," he said, "and that's my final offer."

She let her lips roam over his face. "You're a hard bargainer, Dr. Shaffer."

"You better believe it."

"If that's your final offer, I suppose I'll have to accept it," she murmured and sighed again as his searching mouth took hers.

*   *   *   *   *

COMING
NEXT MONTH

#309 THE ICE CREAM MAN—Kathleen Korbel

Could the handsome new ice cream man in Jenny Lake's neighborhood be
selling more than chocolate and vanilla? She didn't want to believe the rumors
that he could be a drug dealer, but there was something strange about an ice
cream man who clearly disliked children. For undercover detective Nick
Barnett, this assignment was unrelieved misery—except for Jenny, who was
charmingly capable of making his life sweeter than it had ever been.

#310 SOMEBODY'S BABY—Marilyn Pappano

Giving up custody of her infant daughter to care for her critically ill son had
been Sarah Lawson's only choice. Now, a year later, she was back to claim
Katie from her father, Daniel Ryan, as per their custody arrangement. But
Daniel had no intention of giving up his adorable daughter, agreement or not!
Then, through their mutual love for Katie, they began to learn that the only
arrangement that really worked was to become a family—forever.

#311 MAGIC IN THE AIR—Marilyn Tracy

Bound by events in the past, Jeannie Donnelly tried to avenge an ancient
wrong and become the rightful leader of the Natuwa tribe. But she found her
plans blocked by Michael O'Shea, surrogate son of the man she had to
depose. The pain of yesterday could only be put to rest when they learned
that trust and compromise—and love—were the only keys to the future.

#312 MISTRESS OF FOXGROVE—Lee Magner

The hired help didn't mix with the upper class—at least that was what stable
manager Beau Lamond believed before he fell for heiress Elaine Faust.
Surrounded by malicious gossip and still hurting from a shattered marriage,
Elaine turned to Beau for the friendship and love she so desperately needed.
But Beau was not what he seemed, and the secret he was keeping might
destroy their burgeoning love.

AVAILABLE THIS MONTH:

Indulge a Little, Give a Lot

To receive your free gift send us the required number of proofs-of-purchase from any specially marked "Indulge A Little" Harlequin or Silhouette book with the Offer Certificate properly completed, plus a cheque or money order (do not send cash) to cover postage and handling payable to Harlequin/Silhouette "Indulge A Little, Give A Lot" Offer. We will send you the specified gift.

Mail-in-Offer

Item:	OFFER CERTIFICATE			
	A. Collector's Doll	B. Soaps in a Basket	C. Potpourri Sachet	D. Scented Hangers
# of Proofs-of-Purchase	18	12	6	4
Postage & Handling	$3.25	$2.75	$2.25	$2.00
Check One				

Name _____

Address _____ Apt. # _____

City _____ State _____ Zip _____

Indulge
A LITTLE
GIVE
A LOT

ONE PROOF OF PURCHASE

To collect your free gift by mail you must include the necessary number of proofs-of-purchase plus postage and handling with offer certificate.

SSE-1

Harlequin®/Silhouette®

Mail this certificate, designated number of proofs-of-purchase and check or money order for postage and handling to:

INDULGE A LITTLE
P.O. Box 9055 Buffalo, N.Y. 14269-9055